Once upon a tim
In a random Stoc
Began an unconve........ ..... story
That was written in the stars

The war of the roses may not be over
In fact with these two, it's just the start
But it seems despite their constant battles
They have won each other's hearts

A rugged Yorkshire caveman,
And a feisty Lancashire lass.
Their differences go beyond their counties
But they have found a love that lasts

Together with their parents
They'd like to invite you to
A celebration of their love
When they finally say 'I do'

On the 11th of November this year
Please join us for a day of joy and laughter
Where 'The Claytards' will write their next
chapter
And start their 'happily ever after'

Dear Reader

March winds blow us good reading this month! Christine Adams' SMOOTH OPERATOR shows the useful as well as glamorous side of plastic surgery, while Drusilla Douglas has two sisters apparently after the same man in RIVALS FOR A SURGEON. Abigail Gordon's A DAUNTING DIVERSION is a touching story of a twin left alone to find a new path in life, and we welcome back Margaret Holt with AN INDISPENSABLE WOMAN. Enjoy!

The Editor

Margaret Holt trained as a nurse and midwife in Surrey, and has practised midwifery for thirty-five years. She moved to Manchester when she married, and has two graduate daughters. Now widowed, she enjoys writing, reading, gardening and supporting her church. Margaret believes strongly in smooth and close co-operation between obstetrician and midwife for the safe care of mothers and their babies.

Recent titles by the same author:

A SONG FOR DR ROSE
A MIDWIFE'S CHOICE

AN
INDISPENSABLE
WOMAN

BY
MARGARET HOLT

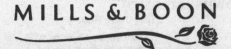

MILLS & BOON LIMITED
ETON HOUSE, 18-24 PARADISE ROAD
RICHMOND, SURREY TW9 1SR

To my dear Dad, Charles Bennett,
and his wonderful wife, Joan.

*First published in Great Britain 1995
by Mills & Boon Limited*

© Margaret Holt 1995

*Australian copyright 1995   Philippine copyright 1995
This edition 1995*

ISBN 0 263 79001 0

*Set in Times 10 on 12 pt. by
Rowland Phototypesetting Limited
Bury St Edmunds, Suffolk*

03-9503-47666

Made and printed in Great Britain

CHAPTER ONE

'CAN I help you?'

Anne Brittain's words were crisp, clear, and demanded an immediate response from the dark-haired stranger lurking in the hospital corridor. She stood in the open doorway of her office, her head tilted up at him, as he smiled and moved towards her. She was unprepared for the intensity of the blue eyes that returned her look and the upward curve of his wide, mobile mouth. There was a jauntiness about him which showed in the thick, arching brows and long, straight nose that gave him a questioning expression equal to her own. Her sudden appearance certainly seemed to interest him.

'Now that would depend on the kind o' help you're offerin',' he replied disconcertingly, in a soft, western Irish accent. 'Would you be Miss Brittain, by some happy chance?'

Anne gave the briefest of nods. 'I am Miss Brittain, yes. Did you want to see me, Mr—er——?'

She paused to give him an opportunity to introduce himself, and for a moment each of them appraised the other. Two blue searchlights were trained upon a slim, attractive woman, whom he judged to be about thirty, dressed in a sister's navy uniform with spotless white collar and cuffs. She was fair-complexioned, with clear brown eyes which he saw were observing him closely, taking in every detail of the sturdy, muscular frame of above middle height, wearing a tweed jacket over a green shirt and corduroy trousers. There was an easiness in his manner, a relaxed informality that puzzled her a little. Should she know this man? While she hesitated, he held out his hand to take hers in a firm grip.

'Happy to meet you, Miss Brittain. You'll forgive me hangin' around, I hope. Conor McGuire, caught in the act of takin' a preliminary recce!'

'Ah, I see. How do you do, Dr McGuire?' she replied, with a formal politeness that he met with a broad smile. 'I believe we are due to meet officially next week, when you take up your appointment in the practice?'

'Correct!' He grinned at her, and she was aware of the confident masculinity of the man. 'I'm lookin' forward to joinin' the team, Miss Brittain, and doin' my stint as resident MO here. Fifty beds you have, then—not as many as I've been used to, but with a well-spread-out country practice to take care of I expect to earn my keep. So what do I call you? It's Anne, if I remember what Dr Sellars said.'

She withdrew a little. 'My official title is Senior Nursing Administrator—'

'Sure, and that's a mouthful to call anybody! Do I say Matron?' he asked, his blue eyes twinkling down at her.

'No, the title of Matron has become obsolete in most NHS hospitals now,' she answered. 'Some of the elderly patients in the Hylton Annexe call me Matron, and some say Sister Brittain, which is fine by me— but most simply say Miss Brittain.'

'And not Anne, then?' he asked innocently.

'Miss Brittain,' she repeated. 'Now, Dr McGuire, I haven't really much time to spare, so——'

'Oh, what a pity, Miss Brittain! And there was myself hopin' you'd show me round the place in the peace and quiet o' the evenin'.' He sighed, though Anne was not convinced of his seriousness. There was an amused glint in those surprisingly blue eyes that looked her up and down.

'Dr Sellars, the senior partner, will show you over the hospital, I'm sure,' she said. 'It really isn't my job to do so, especially as this isn't an official visit on your part,' she pointed out.

'But listen, now, if I were to say that I have a poor old uncle languishin' in the Hylton Annexe, Miss Brittain, wouldn't you take pity on him and me, and show me where to find the man?' he persisted.

'Well, of course. If you'd told me that in the first place, Doctor, it would have helped,' she said in a softer tone. 'Certainly I'll take you over to the annexe. Come this way, please.'

'Gladly,' he murmured as he allowed her to escort him past the women's ward and the little maternity ward, from which a baby could be heard loudly demanding an evening feed.

'The Hylton Annexe is separate from the main building, and we get to it by a covered passageway through the garden,' she explained as he followed her along the glass-roofed corridor leading to a pleasant, single-storeyed extension with accomodation for up to twenty elderly residents. 'You can see the enclosed veranda where they like to sit in the daytime, and through there is the communal dining-room. Most of them have single or double rooms, but we have a four-bedded nursing bay for those in need of extra care—including terminal nursing,' she added in a lowered tone. 'We're proud of the variety of care given at Stretbury Memorial Hospital, Dr McGuire.'

He was aware of the enthusiasm that radiated from this efficient young woman as she spoke, and the brightness of her eyes.

'Is that a fact, now?' he responded, and she glanced at him sharply; his expression appeared to be perfectly serious.

'I expect Dr Sellars has told you that we have fourteen beds for women and ten for men, plus six maternity, over in the main building,' she said. 'We take early post-operative patients from Bristol and Gloucester hospitals, but we no longer do general Theatre work here. However, we do have a full gynaecology operating list here every Tuesday—usually one or two hysterectomies and pelvic floor repairs, plus a few D and Cs. Mr Steynes comes over from Bristol to operate, and also holds an antenatal clinic. So you see, Dr McGuire, this is a busy NHS hospital, even if it *is* smaller than you're used to.'

He nodded knowingly. 'I'll be proud to be a member o' the team, Miss Brittain.'

Anne could not get rid of a nagging suspicion that he was ever so slightly mocking her, but she did not know how to react. She turned and faced him squarely.

'Right, Doctor, which of our patients is your uncle? I'm sure he'll be very pleased to see you, and no doubt a little surprised, too.'

There was a pause before he answered.

'Sure, he'd be as surprised as myself, Miss Brittain, seein' as all my uncles are over in County Donegal right now. The fact is, you see, I said *if* I'd a poor old uncle here in the annexe, would you show me the way to him? And when you were so obligin' as to bring me all the way over here, well—I just didn't have the heart to—'

Anne's brown eyes blazed with indignation. Now she was sure that he was amusing himself at her expense.

'If you think I've nothing better to do, Doctor, than listen to your rather childish talk and waste my time taking you to visit a non-existent uncle——' she began, but he stopped her with a repentant plea.

'Ah, come now, Miss Brittain, and lead me to any old chap who doesn't get many visitors, and I'll call him Uncle just to make it right!' he begged good-humouredly, which only irritated Anne further.

And then she suddenly saw a way to get her own back on this tiresome Irishman. She smiled, and her eyes gleamed wickedly.

'Oh, very well, Dr McGuire, come with me and meet Mr Henry Dodswell,' she said with a demure expression, beckoning him towards a single room where a bald, bewhiskered and very cross-looking old man sat alone, staring glumly out of the window at the well-kept grounds where carpets of early crocuses were coming into bloom.

'Good evening, Mr Dodswell, you've got a visitor!' Anne greeted him pleasantly.

'What? Who the devil's come to plague me now?' was the ungracious response.

'Oh, don't be like that, Mr Dodswell—give us a smile!' she went on. 'Look, this is Dr Conor McGuire who's joining the group practice at the Health Centre, and he's specially asked to meet you!'

'What the blazes for? And what's he after?' growled the old man, not even turning round to look at them.

But both Mr Dodswell and Miss Brittain were unprepared for the warmth of the Irishman's greeting.

'It's me, Uncle Henry, Conor—your long-lost nephew, remember? By all the saints in the calendar! What's the game, you old rascal, hidin' yeself away in this dead-and-alive backwater? Come on, man, stir yeself, and put on yer hat an' coat. We're goin' out for a jar, so we are!'

As Anne stared open-mouthed while Conor reached down a crumpled jacket from a hanger, she saw a flicker of interest in the faded eyes of the old man, abandoned by his relatives because of his bad temper and anti-social habits.

'What the hell do you think you're doing, Doctor?' she demanded with uncharacteristically blunt language. 'You can't just walk in here and remove a patient without permission!'

'Why not?' asked Conor, kneeling down to tie up the laces of the battered pair of outdoor shoes that he had eased on to Mr Dodswell's bony feet while the patient thrust his arms into the sleeves of the jacket. 'Here we are on a fine March evenin', and you want to keep me uncle indoors? Away wid ye, woman, we're goin' after some fresh air, and ye wouldn't be after stoppin' us now, would ye?'

He deliberately broadened his brogue as he pleaded with her, though in fact it exasperated her further. It was the wary smile on the face of the old man that checked her protests and made her words trail away into silence as she watched their preparations for a visit to the nearby pub. Although she remained outwardly disapproving of such high-handed tactics, she simply could not bring herself to stop Mr Dodswell's unexpected treat.

'Oh, very well, then, but you'd better be back

by nine o'clock—do you understand, Doctor?
Without fail!'

And, turning her back on the pair, she walked
briskly back to her office in the main building, telling
herself that she did not want to be a killjoy. . .but if
this was a sample of Dr McGuire's behaviour, he had a
lot to learn about the traditions of Stretbury Memorial
Hospital and its attached group practice!

Yet she could not remember the last time that anybody had managed to coax a smile from poor,
embittered Mr Dodswell, rejected by his family and
even by the other residents of the Hylton Annexe.

Lady Margaret Hylton was giving one of her dinner
parties for the doctors. She always gave one at
Christmas and another in July, after the hospital
Summer Fête; the appointment of a new partner in
the Stretbury practice was a good excuse to have an
extra one in March.

'You'll find time to come, won't you, Anne dear?'
she said in a commanding tone. 'You know you're my
link with the nursing staff, every bit as important as
the general practitioners.' She beamed at Anne as they
stood in the hospital entrance hall, and lowered her
voice a little. 'I do hope that this new Irish doctor is
going to fit in with us, don't you? Graham was quite set
on having him, though I'd have preferred the applicant
from Gloucester.'

Anne smiled back at the formidable old lady with
genuine affection. Ever since the National Health
Service had taken over the local hospital built by old
Lord Hylton as a memorial to his son and the other
Stretbury men killed in the First World War, the family
had had no direct jurisdiction over its management.

Nevertheless, Lady Margaret was chairperson of the influential Hospital League of Friends, and had an honorary place on the Board of Management alongside the Medical Director, Dr Graham Sellars. Her generosity had endowed the Hylton Annexe for elderly residents and likewise the well-equipped Health Centre, built on in the 1960s, with its own small X-ray department and laboratory with a blood-bank. There had been a great many changes in the Gloucestershire market town during the seventy years that the hospital had served the community—a gracious, well-designed building in the same warm yellow Cotswold stone as the church and town hall. Still, its links with the founder's granddaughter were real, and Lady Hylton, JP, clung tenaciously to her informal patronage of it.

'Thank you, Lady Hylton, I'll be delighted to come to dinner on Friday,' smiled Anne.

'Good! Graham and Mrs Sellars will be there, of course, and Clive Stepford with Marjorie—isn't it wonderful news that they're expecting a baby? Little Dr Lester will be on call, I understand, but let's hope she'll be able to look in. I do like to have one woman in the practice, don't you? And of course there'll be the new boy, Dr McGuire, to meet with us all. Tell me, Anne, how do you get on with the Irish? Rather unpredictable, I've found.'

Anne made a suitably non-committal reply, and wondered what she would wear. The light beige wool suit that she wore for church and hospital board meetings would be too warm, and she thought of the green linen two-piece she had worn for the staff Christmas dinner. Back in her flat on the top floor of the hospital, she searched among the not very exciting selection in her wardrobe and finally decided on a pale blue silk

blouse with broderie anglaise trimming at the neck and
wrists. She would team it with a straight skirt in light
navy worsted, and matching court shoes. The simple
lines showed off her slender body to perfection, and
she would put on her single row of pearls and matching
stud earrings. She looked at her reflection in the long
mirror with a more than usually critical eye. It was
high time to go on a shopping trip to Bristol and buy
a couple of new outfits, she decided. Her life might
be dedicated to her career, but that was no reason to
look dowdy. And besides, it was springtime again!

There was a welcoming log fire in the lounge of the
pleasantly old-fashioned house where Lady Hylton
lived with a housekeeper.

'Ah, Anne, dear, come and sit over here with Clive
and Marjorie!' Her hostess beckoned her to the long
settee where the Stepfords sat. 'Graham, a dry sherry
for Anne, please. Elaine Lester has telephoned to say
that she hopes to be here by eight, but there's no sign
of the new boy.' She looked at her watch. 'We'll give
him till eight-fifteen. I do hope that he hasn't forgotten—after all, he is the guest of honour this evening!'

'I believe he went out for a drive, to get to know
the district around Stretbury,' said Graham Sellars.
'He doesn't intend to get lost on his first house-calls!'

'Let's just hope that he hasn't got lost tonight, then,'
said Margaret Hylton. 'It's quite dark, and the practice
covers such a wide area!'

'Where has Dr McGuire worked previously?' asked
Marjorie Stepford.

'All over the place,' answered Graham. 'He's done
a surgical registrarship, and anaesthetics in Belfast for
quite a while. Then he chucked that in and went to sea!'

'Really? As a ship's doctor, you mean?' asked Marjorie.

'Yes, in the Merchant Navy. Something of a jack of all trades, I gather. I thought he'd brighten us up a bit, and he's certainly keen to try his hand at general practice. Have you met him yet, Anne?'

'Yes, I have,' she replied briefly, not wanting to go into details.

'Oh, yes, that's right!' laughed Clive. 'Didn't he con you into showing him over the Hylton Annexe, and then abduct some old chap in there?'

'Never!' exclaimed Lady Hylton.

'Yes, I heard about that, too,' added Graham. 'The night nurse on the annexe said that the old fellow was quite merry when they rolled in after closing-time!'

Anne closed her eyes momentarily, and set her mouth in a very straight line. She had hoped that this piece of folly would not come up in conversation as she felt that it reflected discredit on herself for allowing it to happen. The fact that the two doctors burst into a guffaw of laughter did little to ease her embarrassment.

'Anyway, McGuire's unattached and quite happy to be resident MO, which is a big point in his favour,' went on Graham. 'He'll occupy the flat above the Health Centre for the time being, so he'll be right on the spot if he's needed. You'd better watch out, Anne—don't forget to lock your door when you turn out your bedside lamp!'

There were further chuckles, but Anne flushed indignantly at what she considered an uncalled-for remark. The picture of a spinster settling down for the night was hardly flattering, nor was the veiled implication that she might deliberately leave her door unlocked. Would these men never understand that she was simply not interested in catching a man? That she had given up a prestigious ward sister's post in Bristol in order to return to Stretbury and take up the position she had always dreamed of—to be in charge of dear Stretbury Memorial, the hospital where she had been born and had started her nursing career as a sixteen-year-old cadet, filling in time until she was old enough to go to Bristol Royal Infirmary to train as a nurse and later as a midwife. In former days she would have been called the matron, and the post spelled the achievement of all her ambitions.

From an early age Anne had decided that her happiness was to be found in nursing. She had seen too much trouble in her mother's life, married to an inveterate womaniser, a bit-part actor who had eventually deserted his family for a younger woman and totally disappeared from their lives. Anne's brother Edward was married with two children but, except for a couple of half-hearted relationships during her twenties which had come to nothing, Anne had never been seriously tempted to consider marriage, and she was now totally dedicated to her profession, in which she combined good practical nursing skills with a flair for administration. She welcomed problems as challenges to her initiative, and the GPs knew that their patients were safe in her hands. At thirty-two she occupied a position of authority that many an older woman might have envied. And she was completely happy and fulfilled, or so she told herself.

A ring at the doorbell announced the arrival of Conor McGuire and Elaine Lester, who came in together. The pretty, curly-haired young woman doctor was pink-cheeked and laughing, having given Conor a lift from the Health Centre where he had left his car.

His company had obviously pleased her. He now turned to apologise to Lady Hylton for his lateness. He shook hands with her and the doctors' wives, nodded to his male colleagues, and then his dancing blue eyes fell upon Anne, seated at the far end of the settee.

'Miss Brittain! Has the hospital actually let you out on the town tonight? That's grand!'

And, before she realised his intention, he leaned across Marjorie Stepford and planted a kiss on Anne's cool cheek. She was completely taken by surprise, and by the time his warm lips had brushed against her skin, causing her to take in a sharp breath, he had turned away and was already chatting with Marjorie, asking her how many more months before the baby was due.

During the babble of pre-dinner talk, Anne was conscious of a pleasant tingling sensation on her right cheek where his kiss had fallen. She was surprised by her own reaction to what was after all a mere social greeting, a conventional public gesture. Yet, even as she reminded herself of this obvious fact, she knew that she was gratified by his pleasure in seeing her at the dinner party. She had been annoyed by Graham's silly joke, but she was not in the least put out by Conor McGuire's unexpected kiss—though perhaps a little taken aback.

Lady Hylton announced that dinner was ready, and they all followed her into the dining-room where they took their places at a beautifully laid table of polished oak, lit by candles and decorated with bowls of fresh flowers. Two maids engaged for the evening were ready to serve a meal that had been planned with Dr McGuire in mind: a traditional Irish feast, beginning with steaming bowls of potato and onion soup, sprinkled with chopped parsley.

Lady Hylton sat at one end of the table, with Dr McGuire facing her. Anne was placed on his right, and Elaine on his left, with the two married couples opposite each other.

'Do you have any family in Stretbury, Miss Brittain?' asked Conor in a casually friendly way as they unfolded thick white damask table napkins on their laps and picked up their spoons.

'Yes, my mother lives quite nearby,' she replied. 'She's on her own now, so it's nice that I can keep an eye on her.' She hoped that he would assume her mother to be widowed, and was relieved when he did not pursue his enquiries. 'And what about you, Dr McGuire? Have you any connections with Stretbury?'

'Not yet. Ask me again a year from now,' was the cryptic reply.

'Have you any family in Ireland?' she asked.

'Parents in County Donegal, a brother who's a priest, a sister who's a nun, and two married sisters over here.'

'Really? No other brothers beside the priest?' She smiled, intrigued by the family picture conjured up by this brief description.

'No, only Aidan and myself now.'

She caught his change of tone.

'We lost our other brother,' he continued.

Impulsively she put out a hand and let it rest on his sleeve, just for a moment. He turned to look full into her face, his eyes shadowed in the candlelight; they might have been alone in the room instead of seated at a convivial table with six other people.

'That's the way life goes, Anne. And you've lost your dad, but this old world still goes on turnin'. We have to remember the good times we had with them, don't we?'

He spoke with a gentle sincerity, and she hardly knew how to reply, so merely nodded.

The soup was delicious, and his plate was soon empty. 'D'you think there's a chance of a second helpin'?' he whispered.

She had to smile. 'No, leave room for what's still to come!'

'Ah, what it is to meet a woman who gives a man truly good advice! I can see we're goin' to have an interestin' friendship, you and I.'

The atmosphere had lightened, and he turned to answer a question from Elaine about the Merchant Navy. Anne was left to reflect on what they had exchanged and how much she had learned about Dr McGuire. Conor. It was a nice name, she considered, and suited him well. She wondered what had happened to his brother.

A roast shoulder of gammon was brought in, and heaped vegetable tureens were passed round. Dr Sellars carved the meat while Lady Hylton addressed the company on a familar theme.

'Our hospital has been a refuge in the storm to three generations of Stretbury people, and I will not stand by and let it go the way of so many others of its kind, to become merely a home for the elderly or a glorified convalescent home. Not while I'm alive!' Her ringing tones commanded their attention. 'You all know that I want us to apply for Trust status, to ensure autonomy into the next century?'

'Yes, Margaret, but we'd have to prove that we can deal with a wide range of acute surgical and medical work,' said Graham as he carefully placed slices of clove-studded gammon on each plate.

'Are you suggesting that we *don't*, Doctor?' demanded his hostess in magisterial indignation. 'All right, so patients go to Bristol or Gloucester for major surgery and complex medical tests, but they usually transfer to us within days to be cared for as well, if not better, by Miss Brittain's excellent nurses, and to be conveniently near to their homes. What about you, Dr McGuire? Are you in favour of us becoming a Trust hospital within the NHS?'

Anne saw that Conor was impressed by the forceful old lady, but his reply was diplomatic.

'I've heard nothin' but good about the hospital, your ladyship, but as for goin' after Trust status, well, it's a bit like goin' into the Common Market or Holy Matrimony—you don't know what it's like until you're in it, and once you are, it's not so easy to get out of it.'

There was subdued laughter and wry murmurs of agreement as the guests fell to work on the main course. The vegetable dishes passed from hand to hand, and Conor gave a sudden whoop of delight.

'Colcannon! Ah, your ladyship knows how to serve a grand Irish supper, so you do. This is fit to set before royalty!'

Anne and the others looked on in some bewilderment as he eagerly helped himself to what looked like a version of the humble bubble and squeak. Lady Hylton beamed at him, pleased with the success of her menu.

'I had to consult with an old Irish friend about colcannon, Doctor, and I prepared it myself, with plenty of butter and milk added to the mashed potatoes before blending in the greens. She told me to put in finely chopped spring onions, using the green part as well as the white.'

'This is as good as my mother's,' Conor assured her, bestowing the ultimate accolade. 'It's her colcannon that still tempts me back to Donegal from time to time.'

There were carrots and parsnips as well, and everybody praised the delicious country fare. Bending his dark head close to Anne's, Conor told her that in his childhood a poor Irish family would have thought the meal a feast even without the meat.

'We used to have mash for supper on Saturday nights,' he confided to her. 'We kids sat round the kitchen table while Mother smacked a good helpin' on each plate—and there'd be a little dent in the middle for us to put a dab o' butter in. Aah. . .'

A dreamy reminiscence clouded the blue eyes as he pictured the scene of years gone by—those eyes that had looked so penetratingly into hers when they had exchanged confidences at the start of the meal. She found herself curious about this man who had come such a long way from a humble home in rural Donegal to become a doctor with expertise in several branches of medicine and experience of a man's life at sea. Of course he had been joking about the 'interesting friendship' they were going to have, but he was certainly going to be a lively influence in Stretbury. He had already made a conquest of Lady Hylton, and Anne suspected that Elaine too was impressed by his Celtic good looks and Irish charm. One never knew whether he was serious or not, but his smile was irresistible. . .

Anne pulled her thoughts together quickly, and gave her full attention to the meal as she noticed Elaine's curly head close to his; he was saying something that clearly held her attention, and she was laughing softly as she listened.

The general buzz of conversation at the table continued against a background clatter of knives and forks.

'I think we're all broadly behind you, Margaret,' Sellars was saying. 'Only we could do with a couple more visiting consultants besides Charles Steynes.'

'That's the guy who does a gynae list here, isn't it?' asked Conor.

'Yes, and an antenatal clinic. He has the final say about bookings for delivery,' replied Sellars. 'He books low-risk mothers here, and sends the rest to his own consultant delivery unit at Bristol, plus a few private patients who go to a convent nursing-home. It's thanks to him that we've been able to keep our little maternity ward going when so many GP units have closed down.'

Lady Hylton smiled happily at the expectant mother. 'And what does Mr Steynes say about *you*, Marjorie? Are you going to be delivered here?'

'Clive and I hope so, but Mr Steynes won't promise anything at this stage, especially as it's our first,' replied the doctor's wife, whose five-month pregnancy was emphasised by a voluminous maternity dress.

'Myself, I'd send all primigravidas into a consultant unit,' said Conor. 'It's safer.'

'But we've delivered hundreds of bonny first babies here over the years, Doctor!' said Margaret Hylton in some surprise.

'That's true, Lady Hylton, but I'm not for takin' chances. Besides, first labours can be long and hard, and I like to be able to offer an epidural anaesthetic to a mother who finds it worse than she was prepared for.'

'But women managed without these things in the past, didn't they?' his hostess pointed out.

'Sure, and that's no reason for sufferin' now if there's a means o' relievin' the ag——' He suddenly caught

Marjorie's worried look and checked himself quickly. 'God forgive me, Mrs Stepford, I'm soundin' off like a cock o' the roost!' he apologised. 'Don't mind what I say, just be guided by this guy, what's-his-name, Steynes.'

'I'm surprised that you didn't go on to a consult-antship in anaesthetics, McGuire,' observed Clive rather coldly.

'No, the time came for me to leave Belfast and try my luck at sea,' replied Conor, and Anne thought she saw a shadow pass over his face as a silent memory surfaced. 'But I'm to keep my hand in as resident gas-man here when I'm wanted,' he added, giving Anne a sidelong look and a wink. She responded with an almost imperceptible shake of her head, having no intention of encouraging his familiarity.

When the main course was cleared away there were oohs and aahs as a mountainous fresh fruit salad was served with jugs of thick cream. A cheeseboard domi-nated by a whole Stilton and home-baked biscuits was also set before them.

Spooning a sizeable helping of mature Stilton from the centre of the noble cheese, Conor repaid his host-ess's liberality with a heartfelt compliment.

'I'd like to say to you all, especially to your ladyship, that I've never seen as good a home from home as the Hylton Annexe,' he declared. 'The ladies and gentle-men who live there are enjoyin' a happy old age— well, nearly all o' them; there's always an odd one out. It's got a pleasin' untidiness, if you get my meaning, and I'd be content to see my own mother and dad in there if they ever needed that sort o' care—which heaven forbid. And what better recommendation is there than that?'

Universal smiles greeted this honest praise, and Lady Hylton beamed.

'And a lot of people don't realise that the annexe is the hospital's geriatric ward,' put in Graham.

'Now, now, we don't use that word, Dr Sellars,' Anne reproved him quickly. 'It's called elderly health care nowadays.'

Graham did not care for being corrected in public, and retaliated.

'Which presumably includes letting them out for a pub-crawl under cover of darkness! How did the culprits manage to avoid the all-seeing eye of the Senior Nursing Administrator?'

Anne rolled her eyes heavenwards in exasperation. Would this incident ever be laid to rest, or was it to be repeated and exaggerated for the foreseeable future?

Conor cut in with a chuckle. 'Don't believe everythin' you hear, Graham. Sure, I took out one old-timer for a couple o' jars, and forgot to ask Miss Brittain's permission—'twas my doin' and not hers. But, I ask you, hasn't Harry Dodswell cheered up since his night on the tiles?'

Anne warmed towards him for excluding her from any responsibility for his unconventional therapy. She nodded her agreement, if not her full approval.

'Has anybody heard how Monica Steynes is these days?' asked Lady Hylton, changing the subject. 'Is she any better? Such a burden for a man in his position.'

'Apparently she sees a therapist in Bristol regularly,' Anne told her. 'Charles knows how much she dreads being an in-patient, so he's agreed to private counselling—it's worth a try.'

Margaret nodded. 'Poor Charles, so distressing and

embarrassing. I'm sure he's thankful to escape to Stretbury, aren't you? He told me that he looks forward to his Tuesday lists, and to having a first-rate theatre sister at his side!'

Anne smiled deprecatingly. 'Oh, there are far more experienced theatre sisters, Lady Hylton.'

'Not above *your* standard, my dear. You are quite indispensable to Mr Steynes—and to Stretbury Memorial!'

Conor looked up with interest. 'An indispensable woman, do I hear? That must take some livin' up to, Anne!' Lowering his voice and leaning close to her ear, he went on, 'What's the matter with poor Mrs Steynes? Some sort o' psychiatric problem?'

Anne hesitated. 'You could say that,' she replied briefly, unwilling to discuss the private concerns of a colleague she respected, though everybody else present knew about Monica Steynes' drinking. Conor would find out some enough.

'Uh-huh.' His nod showed that he understood and approved of her reticence. 'So, you are Theatre Sister here, Anne, as well as Senior Nursing Thingummy?'

She bowed her head in mock formality. 'That's right.'

'Good, because it seems that I'm to be regular gas-man for these Tuesday chops. So I look forward to joining in the fun with you and the much-acclaimed Charles!'

Did he really mean that, or was he just teasing her again? What was this man going to be like to work with? Anne came to the conclusion that, for good or ill, there would be few dull moments when Dr Conor McGuire was around. Nevertheless, it would not do to let him think too much of himself, she thought, and when the meal was over and Gaelic coffee was served in the lounge Anne settled herself on the sofa with the doctors' wives. She judged that Elaine Lester would be more than happy to keep the new doctor entertained.

Yet every time she glanced in his direction she met the deep blue eyes, regarding her with a softness in their depths that she could not quite fathom. And it gave her an oddly unfamiliar flutter of the heart.

CHAPTER TWO

WHEN Anne went into her office at five minutes to eight on the following Monday morning the usual series of problems awaited her. Two male patients were being transferred from Bristol after surgery three days previously, and the men's ward was short-staffed, due to the senior staff nurse being off sick with a sore throat and raised temperature. Sister Louise Barr of the women's ward had angrily rebuked the part-time staff nurse on night duty who had failed to notice a leaking pipe in the sluice overnight, resulting in a serious flood. The night nurse had gone home in tears, and her irate husband was now on the telephone demanding an apology. And Maternity had run out of disposable nappies over the weekend.

'I said we should have stuck to terry napkins,' muttered the nursing auxiliary who had come to Miss Brittain's office to collect a packet of twenty disposable that Anne kept for emergencies. 'They're better for the babies' bottoms, and ever so much cheaper in the long run.'

Anne felt obliged to reply that they had had to move with the times and use the more convenient type. She cut short the auxiliary's grumbles about extravagance and handed over the packet without further comparisons. She then studied the staff duty roster for the day; an extra pair of hands would be needed on the men's ward when the two new patients arrived by ambulance, but Sister Barr would strongly object if one of *her* staff was taken. She had half a dozen gynae admissions coming in for operation tomorrow, when Mr Steynes would be coming over as usual. Anne wondered about borrowing an auxiliary from the Hylton Annexe, but decided to help out on the men's ward herself. She enjoyed welcoming new patients, making sure that they were comfortably settled in and introducing them to the staff who would be looking after them, also the other patients in the ward. There would also be the plumber to see when he arrived to repair the leaking pipe; she hoped that this would not be too lengthy a job. And she would have to take Sister Barr aside for a quiet word about upsetting the night nurse and her husband; Anne did not tolerate ill-feeling among the staff, because it affected efficiency and patient care.

When her secretary arrived at nine Anne set out on her daily visit to all four wards, checking the situation in each—not only the staff/patient ratio but the general atmosphere, whether it was cheerful or subdued, tense or calm. In a non-teaching hospital that employed a high percentage of part-time, non-resident staff, Anne was adamant about maintaining the high standards of care for which the hospital was renowned. She had long realised the effectiveness of teaching by practical example, and every staff member knew that Miss Brittain could roll up her navy blue sleeves and carry out any nursing duty necessary—from giving a bedpan to dressing a wound, from feeding a helpless old person in the annexe to showing a harassed young mother in Maternity how to change her baby. As a result, she commanded the respect of all grades of staff, from the two senior sisters who took turns at deputising for her down to the newest care assistant in the annexe. The patients, too, were always pleased to see the smiling,

crisply efficient young woman who found time to listen
to their particular problems, and to set about solving
them; in fact, many would have echoed Lady Hylton's
assertion that Miss Brittain was quite indispensable to
Stretbury Memorial.

Walking across the entrance hall, she saw a Fiat
hatchback sweep up the drive and head towards the
doctors' car park behind the Health Centre. A shower
of gravel was thrown up by new tyres too sharply
turned, and Anne frowned. She recognised the driver,
who would have to be reminded about the five-mile-an-
hour limit in the hospital grounds.

As she stopped to arrange the display of spring
flowers and greenery on the polished circular table in
the hall a door opened at the end of the corridor
leading to the Health Centre.

'Good mornin' to you, Miss Brittain—and a lovely
day it is, to be sure!'

There was no mistaking the voice of the man who
now strode towards her.

'Good morning to *you*, Dr McGuire. So this is your
first day in your new job?'

'It surely is. Aren't you goin' to wish me well?'

'Of course I do. Only for one moment just now I
was afraid that it might be your last day as well. Lucky
that you have good tyres,' she remarked severely.

'Sorry, ma'am. I took that corner too fast, I know—
must have been the thought of seein' you, Anne.'

He looked down at her, his eyes merry, and she was
reminded of a mischievous schoolboy. I mustn't let
him think that I'm a push-over for his Irish charm, she
thought, and straightened her face into sternness.

'In that case you'd better concentrate on driving
more carefully, Doctor, unless you want to end up as

a patient. Now, if you will excuse me, I've a lot to attend to this morning.'

'Thank you for the concern you've shown, Miss Brittain. I'll take it to heart.'

'Good morning, Dr McGuire.'

With a brief smile she turned on her heel and walked briskly towards the women's ward.

'And good mornin' to yourself, kindest o' women,' he murmured after her retreating back, eyeing the slender legs encased in serviceable twenty-denier nylon.

Conor McGuire was accustomed to smiles and encouraging responses from most of the women he met, but it was quite clear that the Senior Nursing Administrator was not to be easily impressed. He returned to the reception desk at the Health Centre, where the patients with appointments were beginning to arrive. The smiling receptionist had already directed an elderly man and a smartly dressed middle-aged woman to the waiting area outside the door which displayed a new name-plate: Dr C. McGuire.

He nodded towards his first patients, took a deep breath, and opened the door on the start of his morning surgery.

Anne spent a busy but satisfying morning, and by the time she went for her afternoon off-duty the two post-operative patients were settled in the men's ward, the leaking pipe had been mended, and a consignment of surgical supplies had been checked and distributed where necessary—including five hundred disposable nappies for Maternity. Sister Barr had duly apologised over the telephone for the remarks she had made to the night nurse, who on her part had admitted to a degree of carelessness, and Anne was relieved to know that there would be no lingering ill-will between them. Her duties done, she decided to go out and do a little local shopping.

It was a beautiful fresh March day, the sky was a cloudless blue, and a stiff breeze wafted across the Gloucestershire countryside, up from the Severn estuary. The first daffodils were shooting green leaves, and would soon be a blaze of gold in the hospital grounds. Anne walked with a spring in her step, rejoicing that she lived so close to the country, enjoying the changing seasons at close hand; how lucky she was! After a good brisk walk around the shops, a visit to the library and a chat with the inevitable former patients she always seemed to meet, she decided to call at her mother's little bungalow.

Mrs Brittain was a home-help, and could give Anne useful information about the progress of discharged patients. She was very proud of her daughter, and shared Lady Hylton's views about her indispensability to the hospital. If Mrs Brittain ever secretly hoped that Anne would one day meet and marry a nice doctor and have children, she was too wise to mention it. She knew Anne's views about marriage, likewise her dedication to her work.

'That was delicious, Mother!' Anne set down her cup and saucer and the tea-plate which had held two newly baked scones. 'I'm revictualled before going back on duty. It's your Flower Guild meeting at St Joseph's this evening, isn't it?'

'No, dear, not tonight. I'm popping out to see a couple of my old people who are on their own and could do with the sight of a friendly face,' replied her mother, who knew that Anne did not approve of all the extra unpaid hours she put in for her elderly 'clients'.

'Now, Mother, I've told you before about overdoing things, haven't I? You're looking tired, and I don't like you going out alone after dark.'

'It's no distance to old Mr Crawford's, dear, and he does so like a night drink when he's in bed!'

Anne smiled. 'You'd better watch your reputation, Mrs Brittain!'

'To tell you the truth, Anne, I get a bit lonely with only the television for company. It's something useful for me to do,' her mother pleaded.

'All right, but take care now.' Anne kissed her mother with a sudden surge of tenderness, and once again felt bitter contempt for the man who had left this kindly woman for a younger and no doubt more exciting model. She no longer even thought of him as her father these days, and coldly dismissed all childhood memories of him from her heart.

When Anne returned to her office, her secretary had a few messages for her.

'Mr Steynes rang to say that as it's a rather long list tomorrow he'd like to start half an hour earlier, Miss Brittain.'

Anne nodded. 'Very well. Does Dr McGuire know?'

'Yes, and he'll see the patients tonight after the evening surgery. He asked if you'd be around, Miss Brittain, because he has a couple of requests to make, too.'

'Such as?' Anne was sharply attentive.

'He wants to know if he can book a couple of minor cases here,' the girl informed her.

'Really?' Anne's delicately arched eyebrows shot up. 'I hope you told him that he'll have to discuss that with Dr Sellars first.'

'He already has, Miss Brittain, and Graham told him to go ahead.'

'Hmm. Well, I hope he's not going to start bringing in patients right, left and centre when we have such a tight schedule,' said Anne with a slight frown. 'I mean, we never know when we're going to be asked to take quite early post-ops, like those two from Bristol this morning. I'll have to have a word with him.'

'You'll have the opportunity this evening, then, when he drops in to tell you about them—his requests, I mean,' said the secretary, tidying her desk and covering the typewriter before leaving.

Evening surgery had just finished. Conor McGuire straightened the collar of his white coat and looked at his watch. Seven-fifteen, just the right time for some supper. Or should he see Miss Bossy-boots first? His empty stomach decided in favour of cottage pie and peas, and going through into the hospital he ran effortlessly up the main staircase to the staff dining-room, oak-panelled and furnished with a huge carved sideboard that had once graced an Edwardian country house. There were half a dozen circular tables at which a few nurses were already seated; Conor sniffed the delicious savoury aroma—and saw that the lady helping herself from a heated trolley was Anne Brittain. Conor congratulated himself on having made the right decision, for now he could kill two birds with one stone, sorting out an administrative matter while enjoying a meal in the company of a woman who for some reason intrigued and fascinated him, for all their differences.

'This smells good, Miss Brittain! Have you taken all

you want? May I pour you some gravy?' he enquired politely.

'Oh, hello, Dr McGuire. Yes, thank you—that will do nicely,' she replied, picking up her plate.

'I looked in on your secretary this afternoon, and she told me you'd be around,' he said as they sat down at an unoccupied table.

'So I heard. How has your first day gone?' she asked.

'Oh, very well indeed. This is goin' to be great, just what I most enjoy—a bit of everythin', and time to get to know the patients as people living their lives, instead o' case numbers in a row of beds. Now, Anne, there are a couple of patients I'd like to bring in fairly soon, if you've no objection—by the way, is it all right if I talk shop over the meal?'

She nodded briefly. 'Go ahead.'

'One's an old chap who's got a mole on his back that I don't like the look of—found it while I was listenin' to his wheezy chest. He says he's always had it, but o' course he can't see it, and I got the impression that it could be gettin' bigger—a nasty dark brown spot, it is. Anyway, I told him I'd excise it for him— 'cut it right out', I said—and then, if the lab report comes back negative, there's no harm done. If, on the other hand, it's left to get bigger and blacker——' he gestured with his hands '—it could just be malignant.'

'You'd excise it yourself, then?'

'Sure I would. He need only be a day-case, and a local anaesthetic would be better than a general with his chest, so we wouldn't need a gas-man.'

'OK, then, if that's all right with Dr Sellars. I could fix a day next week,' she agreed. 'Anything else?'

'Yes, a pregnant lady who's booked into Southmead Hospital to have her first——'

'But there was no antenatal clinic here today, Doctor,' said Anne.

'No, I met her when I went to see the two-year-old she's mindin' for her sister. She happened to mention how tired she's been feelin', and when I sat down for a chat with her she came out with a few other bits of information, like the embarrassin' irritation when she spends a penny, poor girl. She struck me as bein' a bit big for her dates, so——'

'So you wondered about gestational diabetes?' prompted Anne.

'Exactly. So could we have her in for a twenty-four-hour blood sugar profile?'

'Isn't that a bit early? I'll ask the community midwife to call and test her urine first,' said Anne. 'And, if she's booked for Southmead, she should go there for any in-patient care.'

'My dear girl, what sort of a GP do you take me for? I had my medistix with me, and asked her to produce a specimen for me. Full o' sugar, it was.'

'Oh, I see,' said Anne, slightly taken aback.

'So why don't we do a BSP here, and save her all the hassle o' spendin' twenty-four hours in a hospital fifteen miles away?'

'Yes, of course.' Anne could not fault his reasoning, nor the saving of time and expense by his on-the-spot testing of the patient's urine. She was also impressed by his thorough examination of the old man's chest which had led to the discovery of the potentially dangerous mole.

'No problem, Doctor,' she said quickly. 'Just mention it to Mr Steynes tomorrow, and I'll fix a date for the BSP as soon as possible.'

'Good girl. That just leaves Victoria. Not quite so

easily solved, but just as urgent, really.'

'Who on earth is Victoria?' asked Anne, wide-eyed.

'A very sweet and charmin' old lady who lives alone in one of those cottages on the Rockhampton Road,' he told her. 'She's managed to look after herself up to now, but the time's come for her to be properly cared for. Could we have her into the Hylton Annexe for assessment, and maybe keep her with us? She's lived in this area for most of her life.'

'Ah, I'm afraid that's not the way the annexe works,' Anne explained. 'If this old lady is living in a state of neglect, you must get in touch with Dr Sulliman, the consultant for elderly health care, and he'll do a home visit and arrange for her to be admitted to an assessment unit in Bristol. They'll sort out what sort of care she needs—county council home or nursing-home or hospital—and transfer her accordingly. By what you say, it could quite likely be the Hylton Annexe if she's a Stretbury resident.'

She smiled as she spoke but there was no answering warmth in Conor's eyes; their blueness held a cold look that she had not seen before and when he spoke his voice had a hard insistence.

'I want this lady admitted directly to the annexe— no, don't tell me all about the rules, but just listen for a minute. I went to see Victoria today because a neighbour had telephoned the Health Centre. She hadn't seen Victoria about lately, so she went to the cottage and found the old lady badly bruised after a fall. She hadn't been feedin' herself properly, either. When I called I found the sweetest person I've met in Stretbury so far, but she'll deteriorate rapidly if somethin' isn't done very soon. I promised her I'd have her brought in to us, Anne, and quickly.'

'I'm trying to explain to you, Doctor, that you have to consult Dr Sulliman in this sort of situation, and he'll do all the arranging. He's very reasonable and caring—he'd go to see this old lady tonight if you urgently requested it,' Anne assured him patiently.

Instead of replying, he asked her abruptly if she wanted any dessert.

'Baked apples or ice-cream, Anne?'

'I'll just have a cup of tea, thanks,' she answered.

He got up and helped himself to a baked apple with custard. He brought it to the table with two cups of tea.

'Do you take sugar, Anne?'

'No, thanks.'

'Right.' He picked up his dessert spoon. 'Now then, Miss Senior Nursin' Administrator Brittain, I've got somethin' to tell you. I'm not goin' to let this lovely, intelligent lady go into any geriatric assessment unit in Bristol or anywhere else. It would upset her, and I'm not havin' it, d'ye see? The poor darlin' is comin' in *here*, to the Hylton Annexe.'

Anne stared across the table in blank astonishment.

'I beg your pardon, Dr McGuire, but it's not in my hands, just as it's not in yours. Just go and telephone Dr Sulliman with your problem, and let *him* explain to you about the routine procedure. He'll visit this lady and admit her to an available bed for assessment, as I've already said.'

Conor's expression was as black as a thundercloud, and there was a dangerous edge to his voice as he replied.

'Damnation take the routine procedure! Rules have to be bent in the name o' humanity, for heaven's sake!'

Heads were turning in their direction, and Anne became seriously annoyed.

'Don't raise your voice to me, Doctor,' she said icily. 'For one thing, I don't listen to people who shout, and for another, I simply haven't the authority to admit some patient you've taken a liking to, however commendable. And I might add that if you think you can get your own way by throwing a fit of temper, you'll have to think again and learn to use the proper channels. Excuse me, I must go and see the two post-ops in the men's ward.'

She pushed away the teacup and rose abruptly.

'Anne! Just sit down and listen to me, will you? Please?'

'Good evening, Dr McGuire.'

And she was gone, leaving him sitting at the table with two cups of tea and several curious stares from around the room.

Anne was on duty at a quarter to eight the following morning in order to be ready for the operating list at eight-thirty. Changing into a blue cotton theatre dress and white plimsolls and tucking her hair under a blue elasticated paper cap, she put on a surgical mask and went into the little operating theatre. She plugged in the suction pump and diathermy, checked the overhead lamp, and set out the paper packets containing sterile theatre gowns and gloves, making sure that there were sufficient pairs of size eight and a half for Mr Steynes.

'Good mornin', Miss Brittain. Have you slept well?'

She gave a start, and turned round quickly. Conor McGuire stood in the doorway, freshly shaved and smiling as if he was as pleased with life as the birds singing outside. He had changed into a blue theatre tunic, trousers and cap, and had been checking the anaesthetic trolley and drugs in the small room adjoining the theatre.

'Good morning, Dr McGuire,' she replied coolly, without stopping her preparation routine, though inwardly she felt that treacherous flutter again. What was it about this man that had such a disturbing effect on her concentration? she thought crossly as he continued to stand there, looking at her with a certain hesitation, as if trying to find the right words to express what he wanted to say.

He cleared his throat. 'We've got a fair old list to get through this mornin', Anne, and it's my first session as gas-man here. I hope we'll work together well, and—and be friends.'

'Is there any reason why we should not?' she returned, her clear brown eyes wide and direct as she raised her head to face him for a long moment, before lowering her gaze and attending to the work in hand.

This did not seem to satisfy him, for he continued to regard her intently, his head on one side, as if he wanted to read her true thoughts.

'Would it help if I were to apologise for what I said last night?' he offered. 'Because, believe me, Anne, I'm heartily sorry about it—my attitude was all wrong, though I meant what I said about Victoria—but I don't like bein' out o' friendship wid ye, Anne, and that's a fact!'

'Thank you, Dr McGuire, there's no need to say any more.' She spoke quickly and a little breathlessly, oddly embarrassed by his apology, which he almost seemed to force out of himself, as his lapse of accent showed. 'Let's just get on with our work, shall we? As you say, it's a long list to get through, and our patients need the best we can give.'

He was about to agree, but was stopped from saying more by the arrival of the nurse who acted as 'runner' and a nursing auxiliary who attended to the needs of the anaesthetist and helped wheel the theatre trolley in and out; they too wore 'theatre blues' and plimsolls.

Anne began to scrub her hands and forearms at the long washbasin, and after drying them put on a green sterile operating-gown which the nurse tied up at the back. She eased her hands into powdered surgical gloves, tucking the cuffs of the gown into them; she was then ready to lay out the gleaming stainless steel instruments for the first operation, a radical hysterectomy.

'Ah, there you are, Sister Anne, all ready to begin— what a welcome sight! How are you, my dear? Full of the joys of spring, eh?'

The booming geniality of Charles Steynes' greeting filled the theatre as he strode in wearing theatre blues and white rubber surgical boots. He was accompanied by a house-surgeon from his team, to act as his assistant during the two major operations on the list. Steynes was a big man, thick-set and broad-shouldered, with heavily handsome features and thick grey hair, now covered by a theatre cap. He kept up a flow of amiable chatter about the newspaper headlines of the day, the state of the NHS, his daughter's first year at university and the good spring weather.

'I have to get up before my wife and son are stirring, see to my own breakfast, and get out into the car without so much as a goodbye, such is my lot, Sister Anne,' he told her wryly. 'But it's worth the early start, oh, yes! To drive up from Bristol to Stretbury on a beautiful morning like this, knowing that I shall see my best theatre sister waiting for me—ha! That compensates for everything!' he joked as he scrubbed his hands and burly arms under the running tap, dried them on a sterile towel, and flung it aside for the nurse to pick up from the floor. The girl gave a tiny grimace at his back before handing him an extra large sterile gown out of a packet. With one smooth movement he unfolded it and thrust his arms into the sleeves while the nurse followed him around, trying to tie the back of it.

'Right! Now all we need is our first patient. Is she ready to come in?' he asked with a glance at the door.

Anne nodded to the auxiliary peeping through the window in the door, which opened to admit Dr McGuire pushing a theatre trolley on which lay a pale, grey-haired woman in the merciful oblivion of induced sleep. Conor took hold of the two lifting-poles protruding from the top end of the trolley and the two nurses each took a pole at the bottom end; with a single heave, the patient was transferred to the operating-table on the trolley canvas, and the poles were slid out of it.

'Mrs Daisy Jenkins,' announced Conor, checking the name-bracelet round the woman's wrist with the case-notes which were placed on a shelf with X-rays and laboratory reports.

Steynes nodded without replying, and Anne began to paint the woman's abdomen with pink antiseptic dye, ready for Steynes to make the first incision. She handed him the scalpel balde and the time-honoured ritual was under way. Absolute silence was observed as the operation proceeded—an extensive exploration and clearance of the pelvic cavity from which the uterus, ovaries, Fallopian tubes and all lymphatic glands in the area were removed. Conor had put up an intravenous infusion of glucose and saline, and there were the routine two half-litre units of blood cross-matched in the laboratory refrigerator, should one or both be needed.

It was Mr Steynes' rule that no talking was allowed during a major operation except for his own remarks to his assistant and tersely stated requests—though these were seldom necessary with Anne at his side, working in accordance with his methods, his likes and dislikes with an almost mechanical precision that was not lost on the anaesthetist. It was only as the operation drew to a close, with careful suturing together of the layers of membrane, muscle and skin, that Steynes relaxed and began chatting again.

'A belated good morning to our new anaesthetist, Dr—er——'

'McGuire,' supplied Anne, not looking up from her threaded needles and stitch scissors.

'I can see that you're well-experienced at this sort of thing, McGuire, which is a great relief, I can tell you!' went on Steynes, a trifle condescendingly. 'New GPs are unknown quantities, and I don't pass judgement too soon, but all seems well so far. Yes—good!'

The Irishman's deep blue eyes narrowed a little, and he carefully checked his patient's pulse-rate and blood-pressure, then adjusted the flow of the intra-venous drip, before replying in the broadest of brogues.

'Sure, and Oi try to give satisfaction, yer honour.'

Steynes raised his eyebrows slightly, and the two theatre nurses stifled a giggle. Anne did not look up from the task which absorbed her, so missed Conor's wicked wink.

As Mrs Jenkins was wheeled out of the theatre

Steynes and his assistant pulled off their gowns and gloves. The used instruments were removed by the 'runner', and while Steynes discussed the operative procedures with a politely nodding houseman Anne rescrubbed, regowned and set out the instruments for the next patient. Five minutes later the two doctors were ready to begin again.

'Come on, come on—let's have the next customer,' urged Steynes impatiently. Anne looked towards the doors, which remained closed with no auxiliary's face at the window. She quietly instructed the 'runner' to go and find out what was causing the delay, and the girl returned to say that Dr McGuire was talking with Mrs Fairchild, next on the list for operation.

'*Talking*? What do you mean?' barked Steynes. 'He should be anaesthetising the woman, for God's sake! Does he know that we've been standing around here for half an hour while he has a cosy little chat?'

Another full three minutes ticked by while the surgeon, his assistant and Anne stood by the operating-table, their gloved hands held carefully aloft or clasped together so as not to touch anything that would desterilise them. Just as Steynes was about to pull off his gloves and storm out to see what was the matter the door opened, and McGuire and the auxiliary wheeled in the trolley upon which lay a peacefully sleeping Mrs Fairchild.

'What the hell's been going on out there?' demanded Steynes. 'You might at least have had the courtesy to let us *know* there was some sort of hitch, instead of letting us get gowned and wait around here until you decide to proceed with your job!'

McGuire's reply was as good-humouredly casual as the look he turned on the consultant.

'Beggin' yer honour's pardon for the hold-up, sorr, but poor Mrs Fairchild was so terrified that we had to have a little talk before she went to sleep, ye see.'

'Why was that? Didn't she have a pre-med?' asked Steynes with an angry frown.

'Apparently so, but it hadn't the desired effect, and she was wide awake and literally quakin' with fright,' answered McGuire more seriously. 'She might have lost the tablet through coughin' it out, or when she took out her dentures—it's happened before. Never mind, we calmed her down, this good nurse and I, and here she is.'

He smiled at the auxiliary and caught Anne's eye. She hastily bent over her instruments, annoyed at herself for blushing. Really, the man was impossible! The Tuesday operation list at Stretbury Memorial was known to be a smooth, well-organised example of good team-work, but this self-assured newcomer had jarred the harmony by his lack of respect for theatre protocol. Did the man not acknowledge any rules at all? It bothered Anne to see the way he rattled Charles Steynes, just as he had infuriated her in the dining-room the previous evening. She knew that she had to remain absolutely neutral, because any ill-feeling between staff was detrimental to patient care. She tried to give Steynes a friendly warning glance from above her surgical mask, but all she received was a frown. Poor Charles, she thought, he can't really be expected to see the funny side of life, knowing his private anxieties with his wife. Anne prided herself on a totally professional and platonic relationship with the surgeon, and considered herself to be an understanding colleague who discreetly sympathised with his domestic problems. She was therefore annoyed to see him put out of humour by the tiresome new GP.

The second operation was another hysterectomy, followed by the more fiddly procedure of pelvic floor repair and urethroplasty, which took considerably longer and involved putting the patient into the lithotomy position, with her legs suspended in stirrups. Steynes went ahead with meticulous precision but, although the usual silence was kept throughout, Anne registered a subtle change of atmosphere in the theatre. McGuire's technique could not be faulted; beneath his deceptive ease of manner there was an alertness, a spot-on accuracy and assurance in everything he did, that marked him as a true professional. Anne saw the glances of approval that passed between the two nurses, and she herself was constantly aware of the man's presence, an indefinable strength of character and purpose that emanated from his loose-limbed frame.

At a quarter past eleven they stopped for coffee in an adjoining office and the assistant surgeon left them, not being needed for the laparoscopy and three D and Cs that remained to be done. As was the custom, the auxiliary set out a tray of cups with coffee and biscuits, and the five of them sat down, Charles with a cigarette and Conor with the crossword puzzle in the daily newspaper he had picked up. Instead of her usual sympathetic chat with the surgeon, Anne found her attention straying towards Conor's dark head above the newspaper as the two nurses joined in helping him solve the clues.

'Can anybody think of a word meanin' self-important, with seven letters?' he asked, taking a pen from the pocket of his blue tunic.

'Any letters so far?' asked the auxiliary.

'Second one's "o", and the last one's "s", I think,' he grinned, apparently oblivious to Steynes' malevolent look.

No answer was forthcoming, but Anne secretly concluded that the word must be 'pompous'. She hoped that neither of the nurses would think of it or, if they did, that they would not say it out loud—it would be hardly tactful in the circumstances. She felt pretty sure that the incorrigible McGuire had already written it in.

'This won't do, we'd better get on with the list,' she said hastily, getting up and collecting the cups as Steynes stubbed out his cigarette.

'You're right, Miss Brittain,' responded Conor, folding up the newspaper. 'I'll go and see the next lady while the rest of you are doin' your ablutions.'

Steynes had not said a single word throughout the fifteen-minute break, and his face was like thunder when they returned to the theatre. The four minor operations were completed soon after one o'clock, and Anne thankfully removed her theatre gear for the last time. She and Steynes usually took lunch together in the dining-room on Tuesdays, but today he strode off to his car without a backward glance.

'Comin' for some bangers and mash, Anne?' Conor asked her pleasantly, but she shook her head and made her way up to her flat where she brewed a pot of tea and lay on the bed; her head was aching from the tension of the morning and she felt thoroughly out of sorts.

Men! She thanked her lucky stars to be out of sight and hearing of the infantile creatures. . .

CHAPTER THREE

IT WAS Anne's usual practice to take Tuesday afternoons off after the gynae list and spend the evening
in charge of the women's ward, attending to the post-
operative patients as they recovered from their
anaesthetics. Sister Louise Barr stayed on duty until
five, when Anne took over until the night staff arrived
at eight-thirty. There was a lot of work to do—pulses
and blood-pressures to be recorded, intravenous drips
and bladder drainage catheters to be checked. In
addition to the technical aspect, Anne insisted on high
quality nursing care of the women who were sometimes
bewildered and disorientated as they regained consciousness. A gentle wash of face and hands, a change
of nightgown and kind, reassuring words were also
necessary, likewise the carefully measured sips of ice-
cold water which they all craved. Pain-relieving
injections were prescribed and given to those who had
had major surgery, and Anne liked to have her patients
comfortable and sedated by the time the night nurses
came on duty.

She found it difficult to relax that afternoon as she
lay on her bed; her mind kept going over the events
of the morning in the operating-theatre, and her own
difficult balancing act between the two doctors. She
was quite unable to concentrate on the best-selling
novel she had got from the library, and at four o'clock
she took a shower and made herself a tasty snack of
scrambled eggs and grilled tomatoes. Half an hour later

she put on her uniform and went down to her office
to see the secretary. Because of the early start in the
theatre that morning, she had only exchanged a few
words with the girl at lunchtime.

Apart from the gynae list it had been a fairly
uneventful day, with a couple of discharges and one
new admission.

'An old lady was brought into the Hylton Annexe
under the care of Dr Sulliman,' the secretary reported.
'She is a Miss Knight, suffering from a recent fall—
no bones broken, but extensive bruising. And the usual
poor nutrition.'

'Which GP is she under?' Anne enquired.

'Well, she *was* under old Dr Wolstenholme, but now
she'll be Dr McGuire's, I suppose,' said the girl.
'It sounds as if she has slipped through the net, somehow, and got left off the registers. She's been going
steadily downhill through the winter without being
checked up on.'

Anne frowned. Such an omission would have to be
investigated.

'So she was sent to us from the assessment unit, I
presume?'

'No, Miss Brittain. Dr Sulliman went to do an urgent
domiciliary visit this morning, and ordered her to come
straight in here by ambulance,' was the reply.

Anne was suddenly alerted. 'Have you got her
details here? What's her full name and address?'

The girl opened the heavy admissions book, but
Anne already knew what she would find. Sure enough,
there it was: Miss Victoria Knight of 2 Paddock
Cottages, Rockhampton Road.

So Dr McGuire had got his way. But how? He must
have used all his devious powers of persuasion on the

geriatrician—or rather, the consultant in elderly health care, she corrected herself. Why on earth had Dr Sulliman allowed himself to be dictated to by an unknown GP on his second day in a new job? The consultant had always previously observed the routine procedure for assessment of elderly patients in need of care.

Anne frowned. This simply would not do! She determined to put an early stop to McGuire's riding roughshod over the system. After less than forty-eight hours he had succeeded in alienating one consultant and shamelessly manipulating another, not to mention quarrelling publicly with herself in the dining-room. It could not be allowed to continue.

She looked at her watch. There was time to pay a quick visit to the annexe before taking over from Sister Barr on the women's ward. She was curious to meet this old lady who had wielded such influence over Conor McGuire that he had bent the rules on her behalf and got her a direct admission to the much-praised annexe of Stretbury Memorial.

Sister Mason, the pleasantly plump middle-aged woman in charge of the annexe, greeted Anne warmly.

'Ah, Miss Brittain—you've come to see our new lady, Miss Knight. You'll love her, she's a dear! A real lady, if you know what I mean. I've put her in Room Five. She's rather exhausted after her bath, so she's having her meals in bed today. Tomorrow will be soon enough to meet the other residents.'

Anne nodded. Sister Mason treated all her patients as individuals with different needs, and adjusted her attitude to each one accordingly.

With a smile of welcome on her face, Anne went

into Room Five and saw its occupant. At once her heart seemed to miss a beat as recognition dawned, for she stood in the presence of the former headmistress of the infant and junior school that she herself had attended. For a moment she stood quite still and stared, first in amazement and then in deep compassion at the finely wrinkled face on the pillow, surrounded by a halo of snow-white hair.

'Miss Knight!' Anne breathed softly, stepping forward and holding out her hand. 'After all these years you won't remember me, but——'

The patient's faded blue eyes brightened.

'Little Anne Brittain, one of my most promising children,' she said in a sweet, quavering voice. 'How very kind of you to visit me. Do take a seat, dear, and tell me all your news. How is your brother Edward?'

Anne obediently drew up a chair and sat down at the bedside of the woman who had been in her fifties when Anne had begun her schooldays more than a quarter of a century ago. Now pitifully thin and frail, she still assumed an air of benevolent authority.

'I—I can still recall my first day at school, and how kind you were to me,' faltered Anne, still unable to believe her eyes.

A reminiscent look lit the worn features. 'Ah, I noticed quite soon that you had leadership qualities, my dear. I said to your mother that you would make an excellent nurse one day, because you loved looking after the other children.'

'I'm afraid I must have been rather a bossy little thing,' said Anne with a wry smile. 'Oh, I'm so glad to see you again, Miss Knight. . .'

Her words tailed off as she looked with dismay at the purple bruise on the pale forehead and temple, and she shuddered at the thought of the cold and lonely winter this woman had endured in an old, draughty cottage with no central heating. Anne now vaguely remembered hearing that Miss Knight had gone to nurse a sister at Stroud, and had thought no more about her, assuming that she had left the district. The old lady had probably been proudly independent at the beginning of her retirement, and nobody had noticed the gradual signs of deterioration.

I did not even know that she was still alive, Anne accused herself, and worse still I tried to prevent Dr McGuire from admitting her to the annexe. Thank heaven Miss Knight will never know that, but——Oh, my God! What's *happening* to me, to be so bogged down by rules and regulations?

'Are you all right, Miss Brittain?' asked Sister Mason in some concern at Anne's stricken expression.

'Yes, yes, I'm fine, it's just that——' Anne looked down at the old lady, who had drifted away into a light doze, a contented smile on her face. On an impulse, Anne leaned over and very gently kissed the soft cheek before leaving the room.

'Thank you, Winnie,' she said with uncharacteristic familiarity to a surprised Sister Mason as she left for the women's ward. How could she tell the kindly Winnie Mason of the shock she had received? The incident had pulled her up short, and she saw with a stab of self-reproach that her demanding administrative duties had distanced her from her declared policy of always putting people first. Her former headmistress could have been *any* old person in desperate need of the care and attention for which the Hylton Annexe was renowned, and yet she had argued with the GP who had shown care and compassion enough to bend the rules. It was a lesson that she would take to heart, she told herself regretfully.

And Dr McGuire was entitled to an apology. . .

It was after nine that evening when Anne finally left the women's ward, having handed over to the night sister. Mrs Jenkins and Mrs Fairchild were in a satisfactory condition, as were the two post-ops in the men's ward, now on their fourth day mobilising by degrees.

Anne went into her office and sat down wearily at the desk. There was still a mountain of paperwork to be done following the operation list, and endless notifications to be made and records to be entered in files. She sighed, switched on the anglepoise lamp, and applied herself to about an hour's work. At least she was off-duty now, not liable to be called away at any minute. There was far too much paperwork these days, she decided. As far as she was concerned it ran a very poor second to bedside nursing and was a job to be done only when the patients had been cared for and staff problems sorted out.

By ten o'clock she had just written the last line, and stretched her arms as she yawned and contemplated a relaxing hot bath before climbing into bed. She was about to turn off the lamp when there was a hesitant knock at the door. Her heart sank. What new problem could this be?

'Come in,' she called, as brightly as her tiredness would allow, at the same time putting on her usual smile when help or information was required.

The door opened and there was Conor McGuire, wearing the same tweed jacket and corduroys as when they had first met here at the doorway to her office. He stepped in, closing the door.

'Good evenin', Anne. I saw a light under your door and guessed you were still up. Or rather still down. Sounds Irish,' he apologised.

Anne's thoughts were a little confused on seeing him, but she realised that this was an ideal opportunity for her to apologise over Miss Knight's admission.

'Oh, hello, Dr McGuire. It's been a long day, hasn't it?'

'Sure, it has that, Anne, and I can see you're all in. Maybe I should go away and leave you in peace?'

'No, just stay a minute,' she said hurriedly. 'There's something I've simply got to say, Conor.'

She stopped, uncertain of how to go on.

'Let me have it, then, Anne, with no beatin' about the bush,' he said stoically, assuming the air of a man facing a court-martial.

'I've been to see Miss Victoria Knight in the Hylton Annexe,' she went on quickly, 'and I agree with everything you said about her. She's in desperate need of care, and I'm very glad that she's in with us.'

'And I'm just so happy to hear you say that, Anne,' he answered, with a relaxing of his features. 'I've been so mad at myself for the way I spoke to you on Monday evenin'——'

'No, Conor, don't apologise, please. It's I who should be sorry for trying to stop you doing what you did for her. I just haven't any excuse for behaving in the horrid bureaucratic way that I did, and I—I just don't know why I——'

And there she stopped, unable to go on. Overcome by fatigue and the tensions of the past two days, she was shamefully conscious of tears pricking her eyes. She swayed slightly and caught hold of the desk, gesturing helplessly at the man who was looking at her with a softness in his eyes that she had not seen before. They appeared to be a very deep, unfathomable blue in the light of the lamp and, his generously wide mouth curved in a tender smile, he took her hand, speaking with the soft, musical lilt of his birthplace.

'Easy now, Anne, easy—all that matters under heaven is to be friends, forgettin' and forgivin'.'

'Yes, Conor, of course,' she answered, blinking back the tears that she hoped he had not noticed.

'And we'll work together well, Anne, so we will.'

He was still holding her hand, warming it in his strong clasp.

'Yes, Conor, we must try.'

She looked up and returned his smile, relieved beyond words that she had not completely broken down. Only she would know how perilously close she had been to weeping in front of him.

Conor continued to look down at her, wondering if he might risk saying something further.

'Anne.'

His serious tone immediately engaged her attention, and she looked up into his face. There was an anxious set to his mouth, and the deep blue eyes were troubled.

'A word in your ear, Anne.'

'Yes? What is it?' She felt her heart give a lurch as he placed a firm hand on her shoulder. She caught a whiff of fragrant aftershave, and something else—a wholesome, healthy maleness that seemed to emanate from him like an aura, enveloping her in a warm cloud that drew them together. She breathed in deeply, searching his face and seeing the conflict of emotions held in check—an urge to speak and at the same time a reluctance to utter the warning he felt he must give her.

'What is it, Conor? Tell me,' she whispered, wanting

to know and half afraid of what she would hear.

'Watch your step with that man.'

She stared in bewilderment, not understanding, and drew back from him. The spell was broken.

'What man? What do you mean?' she demanded.

'Steynes.' His face darkened as he pronounced the name; it fell like a stone into a pond.

'Mr Steynes? What nonsense is this? You don't know what you're talking about!' she retorted angrily. 'Why, you don't even know him.'

'I know that he wants you.' His tone was heavy.

Mixed resentment and astonishment welled up within her, and showed in the blazing eyes she turned upon him.

'That is absolutely ridiculous, Conor,' she told him, pushing his hand from her shoulder in a gesture of impatience. 'Mr Steynes is a married man, and I'm only one of many nursing colleagues. We work well together, but there is absolutely nothing, repeat, *nothing*, between us—and the fact that you say there is means that you've got a warped mind——*Oh*!'

Anne trembled with rage and disappointment that their newly-stated friendship had been so rapidly spoiled by this unfounded accusation. Conor seized her shoulder again, and pulled her round to face him.

'Nothin' as far as you're concerned, Anne, I know that much about you—but as to himself, he has other ideas. The man's a lecher.'

The word was uttered in a low growl, and Anne gasped.

'How *dare* you say such a thing?' she cried. 'What possible grounds have you got? How can you know?'

He now had a hand on each of her shoulders, and his eyes seemd to burn down into hers, probing the very depths of her heart. She felt herself trembling and a shiver ran down her spine—not of fear, not of anger, but of a very different reaction that she could not define, something both dangerous and breathtakingly exciting.

'Sure, and I don't know how I know,' he muttered, not taking his gaze from her face. 'What makes a man know what another man's thinkin'? And feelin'? Y'know what they say—it takes one to know one!'

She made an effort to free herself, but his grip on her shoulders tightened as he drew her closer against the roughness of his tweed jacket. Their noses were almost touching, and she felt his warm breath on her skin as he ground out the words in a voice so low as to be scarcely audible.

'Himself and me both, perhaps.'

And then his mouth was upon hers, crushing her lips under an intoxicating pressure. She was seized in his arms, her protests stifled, her breath taken away as she experienced the sensation of his hard, muscular frame against the softness of her woman's body, the uniform dress but a thin barrier to the electrifying sensation. A treacherous weakness of her limbs curiously undermined her powers of resistance and just for a moment she relaxed and let herself lean against him, safely held within the circle of his arms. When at last his lips released hers she gave a long, long sigh.

And then Miss Anne Brittain, Senior Nursing Administrator, suddenly remembered who she was. She made an effort to break free, but found that he was not yet ready to let her go. The pressure of his arms around her was like a statement of possession which he was unwilling to give up. Just for this moment, this timeless space between minutes, her body was his captive, and he held her with jealous ownership.

'Conor. Conor, let me go,' she requested with quiet authority.

And reluctantly he did. Slowly his grip upon her loosened, and she stood before him. Her dress was creased and his hair was distinctly dishevelled, but otherwise nothing had changed; she was still in her office, standing beside the desk as when he had entered. He still stood on the same spot, breathing a little rapidly, and with an expression of utter incredulity, as if he simply could not believe his senses.

'Anne, I—I didn't intend——Oh, hell! Sorry.'

'It's all right,' she said tremulously, adjusting to this return to normality with some difficulty. 'We'd better both forget that this ever happened,' she added, putting up her hand to smooth back her hair.

'All right, then, if you say so, but——Oh, Anne, Anne, what ye do to a man! Where the devil have you come from, woman?'

He turned away from her, embarrassed by his own vulnerability in a situation that neither of them had planned or envisaged, and which had got so out of control. He felt a need to bring himself down to earth and common sense again.

Turning back to her in a swift movement, he began talking quickly.

'Look, shall we go out for a while, Anne? For a quiet drink, maybe, or a snack—or just a little drive to clear our heads?'

Anne marshalled her thoughts together, smoothing her hands over her dress and taking a couple of deep breaths.

'No, Conor. Thank you, but no. There won't be anywhere open now, anyway.'

'Oh, do come out, *mavourneen*, just for half an hour—to get away from everythin'.'

'No.' She was quite firm. 'I don't want to get away from anything, Conor. I've got a lot of things to attend to here, don't you see?'

He looked her up and down, taking in the navy uniform, the directness of her clear brown eyes, the set of her chin, at length he nodded slowly.

'Yes, I think that perhaps I *am* beginnin' to see, Anne.'

'Goodnight, Conor.'

'Goodnight, Miss Brittain. Sleep well.'

And then he was gone, striding down the corridor towards the Health Centre and his flat with its narrow bed.

Anne walked up the two flights of stairs in a dream, unable to believe that the scene in her office had actually taken place—that Conor McGuire had taken her in his arms and that she had actually responded, just for a moment, to the demand of his fierce kiss. For it *had* been fierce, following on his accusation about Charles Steynes. Was the man mad?

And yet. . . She had apologised about Miss Knight, and admitted that he had shown compassion over the old lady's plight. McGuire was obviously a well-meaning man, even though misguided in some of his judgements, and for some reason he had taken a dislike to Steynes. It was true that the gynaecologist's manner could be irritating and arrogant at times, but how could Conor have made such a mistake about his attitude towards herself? She and Charles had known each other professionally for years, and she, like the rest of his acquaintance, sympathised with him over Monica's drink problem. In fact, she admitted that she made allowances for his occasional sulks and ill-temper because of this. Even so, she was sure that he saw her only as the efficient nurse-manager of Stretbury Memorial, quite immune to romantic liaisons or even mild flirtations; he was certainly no *lecher*.

Anger flamed again as she remembered the unpleasant word—after all, McGuire's own behaviour towards her had hardly been respectful! Quite disgraceful, in fact.

So why did she now remember the strength of his arms around her, and the faintly lingering tang of his heady masculinity? He had clearly been stirred by the depth of emotion aroused by that sudden, fierce embrace—she had seen it in his eyes.

And as she drifted off to sleep she wondered what he had seen in hers. . .

CHAPTER FOUR

TIRED though she was, Anne had a restless night and woke frequently, disturbed by the memory of Conor's intensely blue eyes boring into her very soul, or so it seemed. She heard again his words, 'Easy now, Anne, easy,' uttered so softly that it was like a whisper in her ear—in stark contrast to the snarl when he spoke of Steynes.

'Damn the man,' she muttered in exasperation when she found herself once more awake and staring at the ceiling in the pale light of dawn. She got out of bed and went into her little kitchen and plugged in the electric kettle to make tea. She drew back the curtains and stood looking out at the reddening sky above the rounded summit of Sunday's Hill. She was amazed at the way she had reacted to McGuire. Who was this man who had hurtled into her well-ordered life, questioning her authority and making such a ridiculous allegation against a respected consultant surgeon? And followed it by seizing her in his arms. That whirlwind embrace had swept her off her feet momentarily, and had revealed a vulnerability deep within her, a chink in the armour of her self-assurance that she had not known was there; up until now she had prided herself on being in control of her life, both professional and personal.

Well, now she had learned her lesson, she told herself firmly. From now on she would be on her guard against further onslaughts from Conor McGuire's disturbing Irish charm.

Anne drank her tea and nodded to herself as her resolutions took shape. He would learn that she was still in charge of herself and her relationships; whatever he might say, she had settled for a way of life that suited and satisfied her, and she would tolerate no more invasions into her personal space!

Her mind made up, she prepared to do battle with another day's demands on her nursing and managerial skills—a fulfilling role in which the comfort and recovery of her patients was paramount, and problems were challenges to be overcome. She hoped that she would not have to face McGuire again too soon, and her wish was granted for that day. Her only sight of him was through a window, getting into his car to set out on a round of house-calls.

The afternoon of the following day, Thursday, was taken up as usual with the weekly antenatal clinic session. Charles Steynes came over to see a large number of pregnant women from a wide area around Stretbury, the majority of whom were booked in at his consultant delivery unit in Bristol. A relatively small number were booked for the little maternity ward at Stretbury Memorial, but it was a godsend to the other mothers to have a local clinic which saved them a lot of unnecessary travelling, time and expense.

Mr Steynes usually arrived at one-thirty. It was his routine to check on his post-operative patients from Tuesday's list before starting the clinic session at two. On this particular Thursday, however, he telephoned Anne during the morning and said that he would be arriving at twelve, and would take lunch with her.

'Very well, Mr Steynes,' she had replied, suspecting

that he was going to comment unfavourably about Tuesday morning in the theatre. Or he might even want to apologise for departing in a huff.

'We can go for an early first sitting in the dining-room,' she told him. 'That will give you plenty of time afterwards to see Mrs Jenkins and Mrs Fairchild. They're both making quite good progress——'

'I wasn't thinking of the staff dining-room, Sister Anne,' he cut in. 'I need a quiet talk with you, some-where away from the hospital. I've booked lunch for twelve-fifteen at the Huntsman, if that's all right with you.'

Anne was thrown a little off-balance by this. She had arranged to help Sister Wendy Garrett, the midwife in charge of Maternity, to prepare for the clinic, setting up the two examination couches and all the neces-sary equipment, in addition to filing case-notes and laboratory and ultrasonic scan reports for the busy session.

'I shall have to make sure that there is a sister avail-able to deputise for me if I'm to leave the hospital,' she said doubtfully.

'Why, is there anyone in labour? Or any sort of crisis on?' asked Steynes.

'N-No, not at present, though there are two mothers who are nearly due and might come in at any time in labour. And, of course, an emergency could occur at any time on any ward,' she said seriously.

'Oh, let them manage without you for an hour, Sister Anne!' he interrupted. 'Put Louise Barr in charge; she's a very capable girl. I need to talk to you quietly, away from all the constant hurly-burly that you seem to live in. So I'll call for you at twelve, all right?'

'Er—yes, all right then, Mr Steynes,' she said, though she was far from happy about this peremptory *fait accompli*. He might have at least asked her first, before booking the table, she thought, and McGuire's warning drifted back into her head. She could not help remembering his mistrust of Steynes, misguided though she knew it to be. However, she had agreed, albeit reluctantly, to go out to lunch, and decided to act on the consultant's suggestion of asking Sister Barr to take charge of the hospital during her absence at the Huntsman, a well-known hotel-restaurant some three miles up the A38 on the Gloucester side.

She would have to change, of course. She put on a neat dark wool dress and her corduroy jacket with black court shoes. It would be quick and easy to change back into her uniform dress when she returned.

Steyne's Mercedes drew up outside the front entrance on the stroke of midday. He got out to open the passenger door for Anne, who hurried down the three steps with a certain self-consciousness. She had not cared for the way Louise Barr had raised her well-shaped eyebrows on being asked to deputise at such short notice.

'Certainly, Miss Brittain, I'll take over while you and Charles have your little tête-à-tête,' she had said, with a knowing flicker of her light blue eyes. 'Where did you say he was taking you?'

Anne had not mentioned the venue, but had felt that she had to answer such an innocently phrased question.

'Mr Steynes said something about the Huntsman,' she replied lightly.

'My, oh, *my*!' Louise had drawled. Anne could have shaken her.

'Well, thank you, Sister Barr. I shan't be too long away—back by one-thirty at the latest,' she said, picking up her handbag.

'Oh, don't hurry back, Miss Brittain. Enjoy your lunch, and take time to finish your business!' Louise had called after her.

Anne's uneasiness persisted as Steynes drove out of Stretbury and turned northwards on the A38. In less than five minutes they were at the Huntsman, where he took her arm and led her to a table for two in an alcove beside a window overlooking the car park and main road.

Anne waved away the menu. 'I don't eat much at midday, so a small salad will do fine,' she said, though the waiter persuaded her to take a small portion of cottage cheese.

Steynes was disappointed. 'My dear, you must have more than that! And what will you have to drink? A dry sherry?'

'No alcohol.' Anne was adamant. 'I have work to do this afternoon, and so have you, Mr Steynes.'

He shrugged, and ordered a sherry for himself. 'Would you like fruit juice?' he asked her.

'A bitter lemon, please.'

The drinks arrived, with a cottage cheese salad for Anne and a fillet steak with mixed vegetables for him.

'Now, my dear, there are a couple of things I want to talk to you about,' he began as he sipped his drink and unfolded a table-napkin.

'Tuesday morning, I suppose, Mr Steynes.' Anne's tone was blunt and to the point.

'Absolutely spot-on,' he replied. 'I don't know what *you* thought, Anne—I can't go on calling you "Sister" now that we're away from the hospital— but *I* simply won't tolerate another fiasco such as we had in the theatre this week.'

Anne felt that she had to be careful. Much as she respected this man as a surgeon, she was always loyal to the general practitioners who worked in such close co-operation with her, and never took sides in disagreements between her medical colleagues.

'It didn't go as smoothly as usual, that's true,' she admitted. 'You left us without so much as a goodbye or even a thank-you at the end of the list.'

He frowned. 'Well, can you blame me, Anne? That new GP—O'Reilly, or whatever his name is—he was quite insufferable!'

'Was that a reason for you to ignore everybody when we'd finished?' Anne persisted. 'The nursing staff hadn't offended you, I hope?'

'Of course *you* hadn't, Anne, and I apologise for any discourtesy to you, needless to say. Frankly, I thought the two other nurses were rather silly, giggling at that fellow and talking nonsense with him at coffee-time. *His* insolence was something that I'm not prepared to tolerate, and I'm surprised that you don't feel more strongly about it, Anne.'

'I'm sorry, Mr Steynes, but I never discuss the GPs,' she replied firmly. 'You will have to complain to Dr Sellars if you have a fault to find with the anaesthetist.'

'Oh, for God's sake, Anne, you know perfectly well that I'm not complaining about him as an anaesthetist!' said Charles crossly. 'Are you telling me that you didn't even notice the man's behaviour? Talking in that ridiculous accent, winking at the nurses, showing no respect at all for—for theatre protocol!'

'Dr McGuire's technical expertise could not be faulted,' Anne heard herself saying coldly. 'So, if you want to make a formal complaint to the medical director about what you consider his unsatisfactory behaviour, that's up to you. But leave me out of it, if you don't mind.'

Charles Steynes looked distinctly disappointed by her response.

'Well, I won't take it further on this occasion, but he'd better change his attitude or I shall simply refuse to work with him,' he said sulkily. 'Neither you nor I are obliged to put up with that sort of thing, and in fact I'm more indignant on your behalf than on my own.'

'What do you mean, Mr Steynes?' she asked him, not understanding.

'Oh, my dear, you're so innocent, if you don't mind my saying so! Couldn't you see that the man was eyeing you up and down, showing off just to gain your attention? You didn't see his impudent expression when he winked after all that sure-and-begorrah-yer-honour rubbish. And—well, I wasn't going to say this, Anne, but now I think perhaps I should—you'd better watch your step where McGuire's concerned. I don't like him sleeping virtually under the same roof as yourself, Anne, and I'm asking you to be careful, that's all.'

Anne simply could not refrain from smiling when she heard this from Steynes, remembering McGuire's almost identical warning about him. She supposed that she ought to feel flattered at so much concern for her virtue!

He saw the quiver at the corner of her mouth and sighed.

'God knows, I wouldn't upset you for the world, my dear. You've been so sweet and understanding about poor Monica, and you'll never know how grateful I've been—and still am.'

He smiled self-confidently and, leaning towards her, he lowered his voice.

'And that brings me to another matter I want to talk about, Anne, something that's been on my mind for some time. You may have noticed that I've—— Anne?'

His voice rose on a questioning note as he saw that she was not listening. She was looking out of the window with an expression of frozen disbelief.

'What is it, Anne?' he asked, a little irritated by her inattention just when he had been about to introduce a more intimate topic.

Anne continued to stare out in utter dismay as a Fiat hatchback entered the car park and stopped in a space quite close to the Mercedes. She watched Conor McGuire get out, accompanied by Elaine Lester, and together they made their way to the hotel entrance, chatting in a friendly way as they walked. Elaine was smiling happily.

'Oh, it's—er—nothing important, only. . .' She faltered. 'Look, it's a quarter to one, and we've got a busy afternoon ahead. I really think that we ought to be leaving, don't you?'

'For heaven's sake, my dear girl, we're in the middle of a meal!' he protested. 'Whatever's the matter with you today?'

Anne watched the two GPs disappear from her view, and waited miserably for them to appear in the restaurant. She would have given anything to avoid being seen here in Steynes' company by Conor McGuire. In vain did she tell herself that his opinion meant nothing to her, that she was perfectly free to have lunch with anybody she chose, that her conscience was clear— she realised that she still felt a sense of guilt at being found with Steynes. So much for her resolutions of the previous morning!

She did her best to make light conversation, but her eyes strayed minute by minute to the door where the couple would soon appear, and she prepared to face McGuire's piercing blue gaze.

A minute passed by, and then two minutes, and then five. When a full ten minutes had elapsed with no sign of McGuire or his companion, Anne concluded thankfully that they must have gone into the lounge bar of the Huntsman for a drink and a sandwich only—what a relief! She now decided to stay and linger over lunch, in order to give them time to finish their snack and leave. Half an hour should be long enough, she reckoned, and she could still be back at the hospital for one-thirty.

'Are you not feeling too well, my dear?' enquired Steynes in a solicitous tone. 'Time of the month, perhaps?' As a gynaecologist he clearly felt that he could ask this without giving offence.

She shook her head. 'I'm really sorry, Mr Steynes. Yes, I have been feeling a little tired lately, nothing to fuss about. Now, tell me, how is Monica getting on? And your daughter at university? And your son— is it first or second-year A-levels he's studying this year?'

Having firmly directed the conversation away from herself, Anne settled for an apple as dessert, and the waiter brought a pot of tea for two. Steynes was concerned about her poor appetite, but noticed that she brightened and seemed to relax all of a sudden; he did not know that she had just caught sight of Conor and Elaine leaving the car park after their pub lunch.

'Heavens, it's twenty past one!' exclaimed Anne,

setting down her teacup. 'Come on, we must go. The
first mums will soon be arriving for their clinic
appointments.'

As they drove back along the A38 Anne made a
mental note never to go out to lunch again when on
duty, and Charles Steynes was left to reflect on the
strange contrariness of women. It seemed that even the
most rational of them were subject to the occasional
off-day.

Turning in at the gate of the hospital, Anne suddenly
caught sight of the Fiat again, following just behind
them and also turning into the drive. Steynes stopped
at the front entrance for her to get out before continuing round to the car park beside the Health Centre,
and as she emerged and stood upright the Fiat went
slowly past them, carefully observing the five miles per
hour speed limit. Conor looked straight at her, his
blank expression giving nothing away, and Anne could
have wept with vexation; somehow she managed to
return Elaine's bright smile before hurrying into the
entrance hall, from where she flew up the stairs to her
flat and changed back into uniform at record speed.

By the time the antenatal clinic was finished and the
last mother-to-be had departed, Anne was longing for
her evening off; she would go to see her mother, and
perhaps take her out for a drive. She took her leave
of Sister Garrett and a disgruntled Charles Steynes,
and went to her office to sort out a few administrative
details with her secretary.

'There's an antenatal coming in for a twenty-four-
hour blood sugar profile on Monday,' she told the girl.
'She can go into Maternity for the night. The results
are to be phoned through to Mr Steynes straight away.'

'Very well, Miss Brittain. And I've got a note here

about an old gentleman who's for excision of mole by Dr McGuire, a day case. Shall I send for him to come next Wednesday? It would be the best day for us, and should suit Dr McGuire.'

'Just check with him first, please,' said Anne, 'and then send the usual letter to the patient with instructions about fasting from midnight.'

'But isn't it going to be done under a local, Miss Brittain?' queried the secretary. 'He can have a light breakfast, can't he?'

'I'm not too sure,' replied Anne. 'I personally like the patients to be prepared for a general anaesthetic, just in case one's needed. Perhaps you can check that too, could you?'

'We can check with the doctor now, because here he comes up the drive,' said the girl, smiling and waving through the window as the Fiat went past.

Once again Anne's heart sank. This time she would simply have to face the man and behave as if nothing had happened—either the scene in this office on Tuesday evening or being seen returning from lunch today with Charles Steynes. Oh, what business was it of his, anyway?

'Will you ask him, Miss Brittain, or shall I?'

'Er—oh, I'd better speak to him, and get it fixed up,' said Anne, bracing herself for the encounter and determined to appear coolly professional. 'Excuse me, I'll ask him now.'

She put her scarlet-lined cloak around her shoulders against the stiff March breeze, and walked briskly out to the car park. McGuire had got out of his car and was reaching into the back of it to pull out a large cardboard box.

'Good afternoon, Dr McGuire,' began Anne in a

businesslike tone. 'Just a query about that excision of mole you're doing. Will next Wednesday be all right for you? And can the patient have breakfast?'

'Good evenin', Miss Brittain. Yes and yes.'

'Right! Thank you.' She hesitated as he lifted the box, which did not appear to be heavy, and placed it gently on the ground.

'What have you got in there?' she asked, curiosity getting the better of her.

'Ah, now, that would be tellin', wouldn't it?'

Was it her imagination, or did he, too, seem a little embarrassed? She was certain that he was avoiding her eyes, though whether he was annoyed with her or with himself she could not guess. It didn't occur to her that the box might be the reason.

'Oh, go on, tell me what it is,' she repeated, trying to speak lightly, not suspecting that she was putting him in a spot.

'Sure, it's not a commodity you'd immediately think of,' he replied evasively, and she got the impression that he was playing for time.

'Surgical supplies? Stuff for the pharmacy?' she hazarded.

'No.' He was looking like a wrongdoer caught in the act of his crime.

'Is it anything to do with patient care?' she asked, now thoroughly intrigued by this game of twenty questions.

'Er—well, yes, to the extent o' promotin' happiness and allayin' anxiety,' he answered mysteriously.

'Hmm, I could do with some of it myself, then,' she murmured half under her breath. 'Is it for one patient in particular?'

'Yes, but others could benefit—if you let them.' He

turned and looked at her. 'Oh, Anne, you mustn't disapprove o' this—surely you will not!'

'If you'll let me see what it is, you'll find out, won't you?' she said, completely bewildered but very willing to approve if that was what he wanted. 'Open the box!' she demanded majestically.

And he did.

She would never have guessed the contents—a rather elderly female tabby cat, who mewed when he lifted her out and held her against his shoulder, gently stroking her head and rubbing his forefinger under her chin, at which she stretched her thin neck and purred appreciatively.

'Oh, the poor thing! Where did you find her?' smiled Anne.

'Allow me to introduce you to Tabitha, the faithful companion o' Victoria,' he said with mock formality.

'Miss Knight? She hasn't mentioned anything to me about a cat!'

'Well, she's been askin' *me* about her,' went on Conor. 'Tabitha was left with a neighbour, and when I went to enquire after her it seemed she'd been pinin' for her mistress—haven't you, poor old puss? And not eatin'. So I've brought her to stay with Victoria and——'

Anne cut in quickly. 'Conor, you know perfectly well that Tabitha can't stay here,' she said, sadly but definitely. 'There's just no way that pets can be kept in a hospital—I mean, it's just not compatible with basic hygiene, is it? Not with acute surgical patients, and babies in the maternity ward!'

'The Hylton Annexe is entirely separate from the hospital, isn't it?' he pointed out, his blue eyes resting meltingly on Tabitha and herself in turn. Anne's common sense told her that this was a matter on which she really should not give way.

'*No*, Conor. I'm very sorry, but no. And you really shouldn't ask me. No exceptions can be made.' She could feel the colour rising to her face as they confronted each other, remembering that she had been glad when this man had got Miss Knight admitted to the annexe in spite of her initial opposition. And now here he was trying to get the old lady's cat admitted as well! Whatever next?

But this time Conor had more subtle weapons in his armoury. A gentle, persuasive note entered his deep voice as he searched Anne's face.

'Settin' aside hygiene and stuff for a moment, Anne, what would you say if Victoria asked if she could keep her old friend with her, just so long as she's in here, like? This cat's shared the years with her, and they've come through this past winter together, God knows how. What would you say to her, Anne?'

She was silent for a moment, and finally drew a deep breath.

'Look, let's take Tabitha to see Miss Knight, now that you've brought her here,' she suggested. 'I don't know what Sister Mason's going to say, I'm sure—or the other residents!'

But Conor saw the capitulation in her eyes and his mouth curved upwards in a smile of victory, though he wisely restrained his triumph.

'That sounds like a good idea to be goin' on with, sure and it does, Anne,' he agreed politely, then whispered to Tabitha, 'I think we're home and dry, old girl.'

CHAPTER FIVE

ANNE was tempted to linger in the garden for a minute or two as she approached the annexe one Wednesday morning in April. The sky was a clear and cloudless blue, and a soft breeze ruffled her hair as she stood and contemplated the beauty all around her. The army of daffodils that had marched in a golden blaze down the green rise on which the hospital stood were now almost over, but the tulips were coming into bloom, and the first primroses and violets had begun to peep from under the hawthorn hedge. Far above her the tall old trees echoed to the songs of nesting birds among the tender leaf-buds.

Anne smiled and waved to the elderly folk on the veranda. How wonderful it was to see the improvement in Miss Knight, she thought, after a month of good nursing, regular meals and the warmth of central heating. The old lady was walking much better now, helped by the services of the visiting chiropodist. Her eyes had been tested, and she had new spectacles; she had also had a dental check-up.

So many services that should have been brought in much earlier, thought Anne with a sigh. How many more Miss Knights were out there, struggling with failing powers, poverty and loneliness? Too many deserving cases went unaided, often because they would not voluntarily ask for help.

Anne smiled in amusement at the sight of Tabitha, now looking positively smug in her old age, licking her paws to wash her much-stroked coat; she clearly considered herself to be an essential member of the annexe. Another of that man's impulsive hunches that has had a better result than my careful observance of rules, Anne reflected. He's taught me something about priorities, but I must be on my guard or he'll think that he can always get his own way, and that wouldn't do!

She turned her attention to Mr Dodswell, whose outlook on life was changing, she'd noticed. He'd begun to talk about his family, especially his daughter Sheila. Miss Knight's gentle influence was making itself felt in the annexe, and her reminiscences of Sheila as a pupil of hers had stirred the old man's memories of happier times, before Sheila had married a man he'd disliked. With the emigration of his son to Australia, and the crushing blow of his wife's death, Henry Dodswell had become solitary and embittered. His unforgiving attitude towards Sheila meant that she had agreed to the social worker's suggestion that he be taken to an assessment unit in Bristol, from where he had been transferred to the Hylton Annexe as a Stretbury resident. He had withdrawn even further into gloomy isolation, ignoring the other elderly folk and consequently rejected by them. Sheila lived on an estate on the other side of Bristol and seemed to have given up on her father, for she no longer visited him.

Since the arrival of Dr McGuire, however, the old man had gradually opened up over a pint or two, and had begun to see that he had been at least partly to blame. Miss Knight's memories of Sheila as a schoolgirl had awakened a longing to see his daughter again, though he was still battling with his hatred of the man who had 'got her into trouble', as he saw it.

'Good morning, everybody!'

Anne's bright smile was accompanied by a word or two with each old person in turn as she gave out the morning's post.

'Good morning, Matron!' 'Thank you, Sister Brittain!' echoed in response on all sides, and their smiles and nods showed how Anne's daily round was eagerly awaited in the annexe.

'Father Hopkinson will be coming here on Saturday to give Holy Communion,' she announced. 'Yes, I've got your name on the list, Miss Knight. Do you think it would be nice to have the service out here on the veranda if this lovely spring weather continues?'

'Oh yes, Anne dear, that would be very pleasant,' agreed her old teacher. 'This time of year always reminds me of going for walks over Sunday's Hill when the bluebells were in bloom. My dear friend Tom used to pick a bunch for me to put into the belt of my dress. All the young girls used to do that in those days—we often wore fresh flowers in place of jewellery. There was such an abundance of wild flowers then.'

Anne's brown eyes softened as she tried to picture the sweet-faced, laughing girl of sixty years ago, roaming through the bluebell woods with the sweetheart who had adored her. The remembered past was more real to Victoria than the present, though she had settled very happily in the annexe, and was looked up to by the other residents, who sensed her inner tranquillity.

'Is this a private meetin', or can anybody join in?' asked a deep voice as a tall figure appeared on the veranda.

'Good morning, Dr McGuire,' said Victoria Knight.

'Hello, Conor!' beamed another old lady, crippled with arthritis.

'Hi there, Paddy!' shouted an old man who shared the doctor's interest in football.

'Yer young devil,' growled Henry Dodswell, though his eyes lit up.

There was no doubt about the welcome the doctor received as he moved among them, his blue eyes twinkling with merriment. Like Anne, he had a word for everybody—even Tabitha, who stretched herself luxuriously on her cushion as Conor tickled her ears.

'Hello there, Uncle Harry! Are we goin' down to the Anchor for a jar this week? Hi, Nora! When are you goin' to give me an answer? Sure and I'm still livin' in hope that you'll relent,' he pleaded to the arthritic lady who always enjoyed his "nonsense", as she called it. 'Ah, there you are, my dear Miss Knight, chattin' with the boss, as usual. Are they all behavin' themselves this fine mornin'?'

Anne smiled as his eyes rested on her for a moment, and she wondered yet again at the way all these elderly people responded in their different ways to this extraordinary man. In the month since taking up his appointment to the practice he had established himself as a thoroughly caring family doctor, liked and respected by his patients and colleagues; in the case of Dr Lester Anne suspected a stronger attachment on her side. The Tuesday gynae lists had settled into an accepted routine, and Charles Steynes had had to recognise the worth of a first-class anaesthetist, much as he continued to dislike the man's easy, unhurried manner of working. At the coffee-breaks Steynes now retired to a visitors' waiting-room instead of sitting with McGuire and the theatre nurses, but when he had asked Anne to share this place of refuge with him she had politely declined, to his chagrin. She hoped that

Conor had noticed, but he had given no sign.

Now Conor was sitting beside Mr Dodswell, deep in earnest talk with the old man. Anne took a seat by Miss Knight, whose conversation she always enjoyed. Victoria loved to recall her twenties, the happiest time of her life, when she had been courted by a young poet and playwright; she had been the inspiration for his work that had been acclaimed as full of early promise in those far-off golden summers of the 1930s. As she talked about those times her eyes shone and her transparently pale skin flushed a soft pink—the events she described might have happened yesterday instead of more than half a century ago. And then, as so often happened, she lost the thread of her narrative and drifted into a light doze in mid-sentence.

Anne looked up to see Conor standing above her.

'Well now, Miss Brittain, my uncle Harry needs some information,' he said. 'Maybe we could toddle into the office when you've a minute to spare?'

Anne wondered what unorthodox scheme he had in mind this time, but she smiled tolerantly and walked with him into the office of the annexe, out of earshot of the residents. Conor came straight to the point.

'Uncle Harry wants to see his daughter again, poor old devil.'

Anne nodded. 'Yes, that's the impression I've been getting lately, too,' she agreed. 'But will she come to see him? I'm not at all sure, remembering how he behaved towards her. I asked her to come and see me, you know, and she actually told me that he'd said he never wanted to see her again.'

'Yes, Anne, he's told me the whole sad tale,' Conor cut in.

'But only his side of it,' she frowned.

'Not really, Anne. He's seein' his own faults more and more as he thinks it over. Listen, I've said that I'll get in touch with Sheila and ask her to come and visit him. He can't remember the number of her flat, so could I get it from his case-notes? She'll be down as his next of kin. Ah, it would be nice if the pair o' them could kiss and make up—time isn't on his side, is it?'

'It *would* be nice, of course, but don't bank on it, Conor,' warned Anne, a sombre expression darkening her brow. 'It isn't always so easy to forget and forgive. You can try, but it will be up to Sheila whether she agrees to visit or not. I don't think you realise that he said some unforgivable things to her.'

'Nothin' is unforgivable, Anne.'

The words were spoken in a low tone, and she looked up in some surprise at the blue eyes, no longer twinkling but thoughtful and shadowed by some memory.

'That's a very sweeping statement, and I'm afraid I can't agree,' she answered, her soft lips hardening into a straight line that made Conor wonder what had caused so much hurt to this oddly intriguing woman. A cruel rebuff from some man she had once loved? The searing pain of jealousy? No, surely not! He was certain that Anne was not the kind of woman who would allow a man to break her heart and then hold it against him forever; he knew her to be made of sterner stuff than that. But if not a disillusionment in love, then *what*? He realised that this was a sensitive subject, and did not pursue it.

'I see that you and Victoria are as thick as thieves these days!' he grinned, changing the tone abruptly.

'Oh, yes! She's remarkable!' Anne's face lost the

stony look and glowed with enthusiasm. 'What a tragedy, losing Tom like that, from pulmonary tuberculosis, when twenty years later it might have been cured with antibiotics.'

'He was a writer, wasn't he?' asked Conor.

'Yes, and a pretty good one. He'd had a successful play produced, and his book of poetry is still in print. Miss Knight is sure that he would have been an outstanding literary name if he'd lived. It sounds as if they had something really special, she and Tom.'

He shook his dark head slowly. 'And there was no other man—nobody else to take his place in her life?'

'Nobody. He was the only one for her,' replied Anne sadly. 'All her love and maternal devotion got poured into her work, the children she taught. She dedicated her life to them, but now she hasn't got a relative left in the world. Such a pity.'

'And yet she hasn't had an unhappy life, Anne,' he reminded her. 'On the contrary, she's the most serene person I've ever met, and there's not a trace of envy in her soul. Just think, now, if she'd married and had children, hundreds of other children would have missed out on her remarkable gifts as a teacher—and that includes *you*! It isn't for us to question the ways o' the Almighty, Anne, and it's never any use speculatin' on what might have happened if somethin' else hadn't. Victoria made the best of it—even a tragedy. And so must we, Anne—so must we.'

His voice dropped to a soft murmur, and it was Anne's turn to ponder on what thoughts he had left unsaid.

After writing down Mr Dodswell's daughter's address McGuire said that it was time he went out on his house-calls.

'I'll be takin' evenin' surgery tonight for Clive Stepford, and then I'm on call as RMO,' he told her.

'Really? You always seem to be on call, Conor,' she remarked.

'Clive and I swapped. It's Marjorie's birthday, and he's takin' her out to dinner. He'll be coverin' for me tomorrow. Elaine wants to see this Kenneth Branagh film, the Shakespeare one, and I said we'd go, seein' that it's on in Wotton. Heaven only knows what I'll make of it!' He laughed.

'How nice. I believe it's very good,' said Anne, who had also been planning to see the film the following evening, but now decided to postpone it.

'Conor! *There* you are—I've been looking all over!'

Elaine Lester stood at the door, her pretty face aglow with pleasure.

'I've had the most wonderful surprise in this morning's post, Conor—I simply can't believe it!' she told him, her eyes sparkling. Catching sight of Anne, she apologised for interrupting. 'Oh, I'm sorry, Miss Brittain. Please excuse me, won't you?'

Anne gave a cool little nod. 'It's all right, Dr Lester, we'd said all we needed to. It's time I got back to my office.'

'Oh, good, because I'd like a word with Dr McGuire before he goes on his rounds,' smiled Elaine. 'Now, Conor, just listen to this——'

And, linking her arm in his, the young doctor led Conor away from the annexe. Anne watched their two heads close together as they walked down the garden path, Elaine chattering like an excited schoolgirl. Suddenly Conor turned round and looked back at Anne as she stood at the window. He waved, and their eyes met for one brief moment before he turned back and continued on his way. And the give-away flutter of her heart belied her stern reminder to herself that what Conor McGuire chose to do on his evening off was no concern of hers.

She did not see him again all that day, and had gone up to her flat before he returned from a lengthy house-call late that evening. After finishing some paperwork in her office she had relaxed in the luxury of a hot, perfumed bath before settling in bed with a detective novel. The April night was fine but rather chilly, and a breeze ruffled the curtains at the window as she turned off her bedside lamp at ten-thirty.

She did not know how long she had slept when the doorbell at the front entrance roused her. It seemed to go on and on, an urgent, jangling summons that echoed throughout the small hospital. Anne sat up in alarm as she heard footsteps hurrying across the hall from the women's ward as Night Sister Pilgrim went to open the door. Then the hall was full of voices, especially that of a woman sobbing hysterically.

Anne switched on the light; her bedside clock said ten minutes past twelve. Without hesitation she leapt out of bed, threw on her blue dressing-gown, thrust her feet into slippers and hurried down the two flights of stairs to the entrance hall, where a confused scene met her. Sister Pilgrim and an auxiliary were trying to calm a distraught woman who was obviously due to have a baby. She had a dishevelled appearance, with blood on her clothes and hair, and a smear of dirt across her face.

'He's dead, I tell you, he's *dead*!' she cried out, her face contorted with pain and fear. 'Oh, my God, my husband's been killed—oh, God, oh, God!'

A man and a woman whom Anne recognised as a Stretbury couple were both trying to explain what had happened.

'One at a time, please,' requested Anne, gently but firmly. '*You* tell me,' she said to the man.

'There's been a car crash up on the A38, Sister,' he told her breathlessly. 'This lady's husband's car was hit—he's still in it——'

'She says he's dead,' cut in the wife.

'It seems they were hit by another car coming in the opposite direction on the wrong side of the road,' went on the husband. 'There were one or two men in it, she's not sure, but—er—no sign of life after the crash. She was the only conscious survivor, and managed to climb out of the car and run off to the first house she came to, which happened to be ours. I sent out a 999 call straight away, and we've brought her here.'

'The poor girl's having a baby,' said his wife. 'She was on her way to hospital in Bristol when this happened.'

The night sister had by now managed to quieten the pregnant woman and remove her soiled coat. She had given her name as Mrs Janet Taylor, and confirmed that her husband had been driving her to hospital because her labour had begun at around eleven o'clock.

'Go and ask the midwife on duty to come and attend to her,' Anne told the auxiliary, 'and somebody call Dr McGuire.'

At that moment Conor appeared, hurrying up the corridor from the Health Centre; he had hastily dressed and thrown a white coat over his clothes. He listened attentively to a brief repeated account of what had happened.

'Yes, I thought I heard a police car a few minutes ago—on its way followin' the 999 call, I presume.' He nodded. 'When was it sent out? About midnight? So an ambulance should be goin' there as well? How far does it have to come?'

'Eight miles from the station at Wotton, that's if there's one available,' replied Anne in a low voice. 'There áre only two. In a wide rural area like this you can't always count on getting one in less than twenty minutes.'

McGuire was thinking quickly. 'Look, the midwife on duty can take charge o' this poor girl,' he said. 'And I'd better go and take a look at the—the accident. If they have to wait that long for an ambulance, there might be somethin' I can do meanwhile. Can I get my hands on some first-aid equipment, and maybe some blankets?' He glanced at Anne. 'Could you come too, Miss Brittain? Two heads and two pairs o' hands could make a difference.'

'Yes, all right. Go and get your car out, and bring it round to the front,' Anne rapped out. 'I'll follow on in my own car. Sister Pilgrim, get the emergency box from the treatment-room, will you? I'll take some intravenous fluid and giving-sets from the women's ward. Shall we need morphine, do you think? I'll take a couple of ampoules, just in case.'

Turning to the auxiliary, she ordered her to fetch blankets, towels and a couple of pillows from the linen cupboard.

'You'll need to get some clothes on, won't you?' murmured McGuire as he went to get his car out.

Anne flew back up the stairs to her room where she speedily dressed, pulling on her uniform dress and grabbing her jacket. When she returned she found

Sister Page, the midwife, having difficulty in persuading Janet to go with her to the maternity ward. The contractions were coming every ten minutes, and were getting stronger—it was her first baby—but she wanted to go back to see her husband before the ambulance arrived to take him away.

Conor had returned, and went to speak to Janet as she sat beside Sister Page on the bench seat in the hall.

'Janet, my dear—that is your name, isn't it?' he asked her gently. 'Tell me, what is your husband's first name?'

'Tony,' she said through tears. 'Oh, let me go back to him, please!'

'Listen, my dear,' he went on, sitting down and putting a strong arm around her shaking frame. 'Does Tony call you Janet, or does he have a special name for you?'

Anne frowned impatiently. Why on earth waste precious time on such a trivial matter when this poor woman was in labour and her husband was seriously injured, possibly dead?

'Hadn't we better be going, Dr McGuire?' she asked shortly.

The deep blue eyes looked up at her in mild rebuke. 'Please, Miss Brittain, I'm speakin' to this lady, so will you kindly let her answer me?'

The request was polite but uttered with an air of total authority that reproached Anne; she flushed and bit her lip, more cross with herself than with him.

'Does Tony have a special name for you, Janet?' he repeated with gentle persistence.

Janet wiped her eyes and looked up at this tall doctor with the soft Irish accent.

'He calls me Jenny,' she faltered.

'Thank you, my dear.' He smiled. 'That could be useful to us. And now, for Tony's sake, and for his baby, I'm askin' you to be very brave and let Sister Page here examine you and give you somethin' to ease your pain—while I go and see what's happenin' with Tony.'

'Oh, let me come too! Please, I want to see him!' cried Janet, heaving herself clumsily up from the bench and clutching at Conor's arm. Almost immediately another contraction seized her muscles, and she moaned and bent over, clutching at her abdomen. The midwife rose and put an arm around her while Conor gently freed himself from Janet's desperate grip.

'No, my dear girl, I'm afraid not,' he said regretfully. 'You must stay here and have your baby. No, Janet, listen—I'll come back and tell you about Tony. I'll tell you everythin', I promise, do you hear?'

The words, so solemnly uttered, had their effect, and Janet reluctantly nodded her consent. Sister Page led her away to the maternity ward before the next contraction commenced.

'Right, Miss Brittain, let's go,' said Conor, and picking up the emergency box and two plastic sacks of blankets and pillows he strode out to his car parked at the front entrance. Anne followed, carrying plastic containers of glucose and saline solution.

'We're off, then, Sister Pilgrim,' she said. 'Janet's in your hands now, and I know you'll do your best for her. Phone through to Bristol to tell them what's happened, and say that we're keeping her here. Ask for her details—blood group and any special instructions about delivery.'

'Right-o, Miss Brittain. Good luck, and I hope you don't find anything too—too bad,' replied the night sister, repressing a shudder.

Conor put the equipment into the boot of his car, got in, and with a scrunching of tyres on gravel he pulled out of the drive and headed for the main road, in the direction of the A38, about three-quarters of a mile away.

Anne got out her car, and as she was about to move off the auxiliary nurse ran out with a Thermos flask and two plastic cups.

'Coffee, Miss Brittain, with sugar—I hope that's all right?'

'Wonderful,' replied Anne gratefully.

A police car was already parked at the side of the road when Conor arrived at the scene, and a couple of officers were examining the two wrecked cars on the left side of the A38, facing towards Bristol. Their position fitted with Janet's description of the accident, the Taylors' car having been hit sideways-on by a smaller oncoming car that had swerved over to the wrong side of the road. They were both badly damaged at the site of impact, and were now tipped at a crazy angle. The drivers were still in their seats, having taken the brunt of the collision, and there was an ominous silence, broken only by a faint, intermittent moan from the man at the driver's seat in the smaller car. A shaking, white-faced youth of about eighteen was sitting at the side of the road, staring stupidly into space.

Conor parked behind the police car on a flat, grassy verge backed by a thick hedge beyond which were fields. He got out and spoke to the officers, introducing himself as a doctor.

'Glad to see you, Doc, though the sooner the ambulance gets here, the better,' said the senior officer. 'If it had been head-on, I doubt if anybody would have stood a chance. I'm not very happy about the chap in the car that was hit—his head must have met the roof of the car with one hell of a crack, and he's right out.' He grimaced meaningly.

'Uh-huh. And the other car, who's in that?' asked Conor, taking the box and blankets out of the boot as Anne arrived and parked her car behind his; she quickly got out and joined them.

'Driver's trapped in the seat, but conscious—seems to be in a fair bit of pain,' replied the police officer. 'The young chap was on the back seat, sprawled out and stinking of alcohol—we got him out easily enough. Not much doubt that drink played a big part in this,' he ended, in a tone of angry contempt.

'Wh-what happened?' groaned the youth, lifting unfocused eyes towards them from where he sat shivering at the roadside; he was clearly shocked as well as drunk.

'You tell *us*, mate,' the officer answered grimly. 'The car you were in ran into another, and people are seriously injured. Who's the man in the driver's seat of your vehicle?'

'It's me dad. *Dad*!' wailed the young man in growing realisation of the horror that had taken place. 'Oh, my Gawd!'

He got scant sympathy from the officers, who were unwilling to let him sit in their car in his condition: his clothes were soiled with vomit. Anne quietly wrapped one of the blankets round him and checked his pulse-rate.

'I shouldn't waste your time with him, Nurse, all *he* needs is an Alka-Seltzer,' advised the junior officer with a grimace of disgust. 'It's the poor beggar that was hit that needs your help. Unless he's——'

His attention was diverted by the sight of McGuire attempting to reach Tony Taylor through the passenger door.

'Hey! Careful, Doc, we don't know the petrol situation yet. If there's a full tank and a leak, it could go up like——'

But McGuire, stethoscope around his neck, had already climbed into the crazily tilted passenger seat from where he was examining the inert body at the wheel. Anne ran to the door he had just entered and saw him unbuttoning Taylor's jacket. He then passed the end of the stethoscope up under the man's jersey, and pressed it against his chest. Anne watched, hardly daring to breathe as he moved the stethoscope and listened again. Then he turned to nod at Anne and give a thumbs-up sign.

'Heartbeat about a hundred and twenty, weak but regular. Breathin's very shallow, but he's still with us, Anne.' His voice was quiet but triumphant, and she could have groaned with relief.

'Praise God,' she muttered, thinking of the wife going through the pain of labour with this man's child. 'No sign of consciousness?' she asked, not daring to hope.

'None. He's deeply concussed, and heaven knows what other injuries he may have. He's pinned between the wheel and the back o' the seat—mind you, that could be an asset, keepin' his back straight. Have we got a spinal collar in the box o' tricks?'

There was no collar, but the policemen produced a

newspaper, which Conor rolled up tightly and placed round the man's neck in a double ring, tucking the ends under.

'Makeshift, but better than nothin',' he sighed. 'Get a blanket, will you, Anne? The Lord knows how long he's goin' to have to wait. How's the other driver?'

The police had got the passenger door of the smaller car open, and Anne eased herself in, steeling herself against the nauseating smell. She took the pulse of the driver, who moaned weakly. There was a cut across the bridge of his nose, and his right arm hung uselessly down while his left hand still lay on the steering-wheel. His pulse was weak and thready, and he was in severe pain; Anne suspected internal haemorrhage.

Wriggling out of the seat, she returned to Conor who was carefully wrapping a blanket around Tony and talking in a low, clear voice close to his left ear.

'Don't worry, my friend, Jenny is all right—she's fine. Can you hear me, Tony? Your wife Jenny is safe and bein' looked after. She loves you, Tony, can you hear that? And the baby will be born very soon now. Jenny's all right, don't worry. Your Jenny's safe, and the baby. Good man! There's a good man that ye are, Tony.'

Now Anne knew why Conor had asked about Janet's name and what her husband called her. She knew that even if a person was unconscious due to injury or illness, his ears might still be able to hear and pass on information to that most marvellous of computers, the human brain. Conor had remembered this fact and used it to bring some possible comfort to a badly injured man.

As if in response to the repeated sound of a beloved name over and over again, there was a very slight movement of Tony's head, supported by the newspaper collar. Anne was not sure how significant this was, but she prayed silently.

'Conor,' she whispered. 'I think we could use some morphine for the other driver. He's conscious, but in awful pain, and is probably bleeding somewhere. Also fractured right clavicle by the looks of it—could be a dislocated head of humerus.'

Conor shook his head. 'No way. No morphine when he's already full of alcohol—depresses the respiration and masks the symptoms when he gets to Accident and Emergency at Bristol.'

She nodded. 'Mmm, yes, I suppose you're right, but it's a pity. He's in agony.'

'So's Janet Taylor,' he replied very quietly. 'And her husband's life is in the balance because o' drink-drivin', though not by him.' Conor's expression was very bleak. 'The two in the other car could end up with a lot to regret, so they could.'

At that moment they heard the junior officer shouting angrily at the young man who had been trying to light a cigarette.

'What the hell d'you think you're doing? Haven't you and your father caused enough damage for one night? Bloody drunken louts—I'd ban you from driving for life!'

He snatched the packet of cigarettes and threw them over the hedge into the field beyond. Anne caught Conor's eye, and they both shrugged; the youth began to sob helplessly.

Anne returned to his father, who was now begging for a sip of water.

'Just a drop to wet my lips,' he gasped, and Anne was now convinced of internal haemorrhage. Knowing

the basic rule that accident victims should not be given
food or drink because of the possibility of a general
anaesthetic, Anne decided to clean up the man's face
with sterile water and a cotton-wool swab from the
emergency box. As she dabbed his skin she squeezed
a little moisture into his mouth.

'Lick your lips on this,' she said, and as he did so,
gratefully, she noticed that his breath did not smell of
alcohol, though the car reeked of it.

'Is my boy all right?' he croaked, forcing the words
from his dry throat. 'He threw up in the back of the
car, and—ouch!'

He winced as Anne cleaned the blood away from
the cut on his nose, but then went on, 'I was fetching
him back from Bristol—I put him in the back seat and
hollered at him to stay put, but he was right out of
control, and the next thing I knew—I couldn't—I
didn't——'

His voice trailed off into a groan. Anne pieced
together the circumstantial evidence and concluded
that this man had been sober but probably angry and
upset by his son's condition, which had caused him to
lose control of the steering, with the tragic results they
now saw.

'Your son is quite all right, don't worry,' she told
him, dabbing his face dry with a towel. The man was
in urgent need of intravenous fluid replacement, and
Conor would have to set up a drip infusion as soon as
possible, she thought.

As she started to wriggle out of the up-ended passenger seat again she heard a subdued cheer from the
two policemen. The ambulance had appeard in the
distance, its headlamps showing above a rise in
the road. Anne thought it the most welcome sight she

had ever seen. Her watch said twelve-forty. Was that all? It seemed an eternity since Janet Taylor had arrived at the hospital.

'Sorry we couldn't get here earlier, we had to come out from Staple Hill,' said the uniformed paramedic who leapt down from his seat next to the driver. 'Right, how many injured?'

Anne was never to forget the speed and efficiency with which these two men, a trained paramedic and his driver assistant, assessed the situation and the needs of the casualties, checking for air-entry, haemorrhage and spinal injury. First Taylor and then the other man were released and slid on to a specially constructed stretcher designed to extricate accident victims and keep their bodies supported while they were lifted into the ambulance. The young man, his face horror-stricken, went in and sat beside his father, staring unbelievingly at the nightmare scene around him.

'Better get drips going on both of these before we move off,' said the paramedic. 'Will you take Taylor, Doctor, and I'll see to the other one. Have you checked pulses and blood-pressures, Charlie?' he asked his assistant. 'And give A and E a call to let them know we're coming, will you?'

Anne assisted Conor as he searched for a suitable vein on the back of Tony Taylor's inert hand, and as the intravenous cannula was inserted the man stirred, frowned, opened his eyes for one moment and mur-mured one word: 'Jenny.'

Anne and Conor exchanged a look of joy, and then Conor spoke breathlessly to Tony, his brogue broaden-ing with every word.

'Sure, and she's all right, Tony, don't ye be worryin' yeself, friend—Jenny's fine, so she is.'

He continued to murmur reassurances as Anne up-ended the plastic bag of glucose and saline solution, adjusting the rate of flow into the vein. She felt the surge of relief like a palpable wave of emotion between herself and the doctor, and her eyes misted for a moment as she listened to the musical lilt of the deep voice comforting his patient. The vague smile that Tony gave him was an enormous recompense for all the fear and anxiety they had experienced on his behalf, and although he slipped back into merciful unconsciousness his brief response was a promising sign that he was beginning to recover from concussion; what after-effects there might be could only be guessed at.

'I'll never take another drink as long as I live,' whis-pered the young man, tears of shame and misery running down his pallid cheeks.

The paramedic told him briskly to get out of the way while his father's right arm was splinted and a pad put under his shoulder. Anne found a moment to rest her hand lightly on the son's arm as she helped to settle the two injured men in preparation for the twelve-mile journey ahead of them to the intensive care unit in Bristol. Conor murmured a few more words to Taylor, and then he and Anne stepped down from the ambulance.

'Right, thanks a million!' said the paramedic. 'Lucky you were around to make a start on the first-aid. Got all your blankets and bits? Great. Cheerio, then—we're on our way.'

And then they were off into the night with their passengers, and Anne was left standing with Conor at the side of the dark, deserted road with two wrecked cars. The police were now engaged on their routine work of checking measurements, skid-marks, and all the details of the vehicles in order to write up a full report of the incident. More police officers arrived and set up temporary warning lights until the investigation was finished and a breakdown unit could tow the cars away.

They walked over to their own cars in silence. Anne felt that there was a great deal she would have liked to say, but simply did not know where or how to begin. She had been so totally absorbed in caring for others over the past eventful hour, but now her own body reminded her that she was chilled to the bone. She felt her knees trembling, and shivered involuntarily.

'All right, Anne?' he asked kindly.

'What? Oh, yes, of course, I'm fine—I——Oh, Conor!'

She gave a gasp that ended in a choking sob; her throat felt tightly constricted, and the trembling of her knees spread alarmingly to every part of her body. To her embarrassment, she shook uncontrollably as she leaned against her car.

'Hey, now, what's all this? Steady now, Anne, steady there.'

She felt his arm around her, strong and deeply comforting. She closed her eyes and felt tears on her cheeks. The night and the stars swirled cold and dark around her, but she was safe and warm, protected by his arms from the darkness with all its horrors of danger and death.

In this delicious intimacy Anne let her head fall weakly against his shoulder. Another sob escaped her, and she turned and buried her face against his jacket, giving in to her unaccustomed faintness for a few grateful minutes; she seemed to draw strength from his body.

He did not speak, but kept her enfolded in the circle of his arms, holding her close, warming her icy hands, gently patting her back like a mother soothing a frightened child. Her trembling began to subside, and gradually she regained control of herself, remembering where she was—and who she was—and who was with her. Heavens, what was she doing? What was she thinking of? She lifted up her head, and her hands flew to her burning cheeks.

'Oh, Conor, Conor, whatever must you think of me?' she said shakily.

He looked down at her, his eyes darkly shadowed; she could not see his expression, but there was a tender amusement in his voice.

'Well, since you ask me, Miss Senior Nursin' Administrator, I'd say you were sufferin' from a very natural reaction to a fairly horrendous experience. It's called physiological shock, you know.'

He released her from the close embrace in which he had been holding her, but kept one arm around her shoulders as he went on, 'And I'd also like to add that you've been marvellous tonight, Anne. You did a great job, especially for that unfortunate driver of the other car. I gather his name was Palmer—and he *wasn't* drunk, then?'

'That's right, he wasn't, but his son was,' she replied, turning down the corners of her mouth. 'Apparently the father had been sent for to fetch the son home from some club in Bristol. He'd put him in the back seat but hadn't belted him in, and the boy was completely out of control. The father lost his grip on the wheel, and——' She broke off with a shudder.

'Pity the poor old dad, then,' muttered Conor. 'Sounds like a hell of a family problem for him. I must admit I could have strangled the boy for all the harm he's done.'

'Somehow I have a feeling that he's going to change from now on,' said Anne seriously. 'Did you see his face when he was in the ambulance? What's happened tonight will stay with him all his life.' She paused, shaking her head. 'That's no comfort to Janet Taylor, though, is it? Oh, poor Tony! Do you think he'll recover?'

'Who can possibly tell at this stage? We can only hope and pray that there'll be no permanent brain damage. I wonder how Janet's gettin' on in labour? We'd better go back now. I could murder a cup o' coffee, couldn't you? Strong and sweet!'

'Conor! You've just reminded me—I've *got* some! Wait a minute——'

And, going to her car, she took out the Thermos flask and two plastic cups that the auxiliary had thrust into her hands just before she left the hospital.

'Just what the doctor ordered!' she quipped a little shakily as she unscrewed the top and poured out two steaming cups.

'Anne, this is a lifesaver, and you're an angel,' he told her as the pair of them gulped thankfully at the reviving beverage.

Suddenly Anne's eyes opened wide as a thought struck her.

'Janet's case!' she cried.

'What?'

'You know—the case that she must have had with her, full of the things she needed for hospital— nighties, towels, things for the baby—it must still be in the car. I'd completely forgotten about it.'

The police had removed the keys from both ignition

switches, but now produced the Taylors' car-keys which opened the boot to reveal Janet's packed case; Anne transferred it to her own car.

Conor silently noted that Anne was her usual self again, well able to drive herself back to the hospital. He had thought at one point that he would have to take her in his car, but now realised that Miss Brittain was tougher than he had thought.

On their return they found Janet Taylor in a fitful, intermittent sleep following an injection of pethidine.

'The cervix was only four centimetres dilated when I examined her,' Sister Page told them in a whisper as they stood at the bedside. 'The baby's head's very high.'

Janet stirred and moaned. 'Tony—where's Tony?' she mumbled. Opening her eyes, she caught sight of Conor. 'Doctor! You said you'd come back and tell me everything!' she cried, sitting up and staring at him in fear.

'Now then, Janet, calm down and I'll tell you—shh!'

He took both her hands in his as he sat down beside her. 'Tony's gone to hospital and he's bein' very well looked after, you can take my word on it, Janet.'

His slow, deep, reassuring tone calmed the woman a little, but the fear remained in her eyes.

'He's not—not dead, Doctor? Tell me the truth!'

'No, Janet, he's alive, but he's got a nasty concussion. When I said your name to him—Jenny—that was when he came round for a moment and smiled at us to show that he'd heard. I gave him your love, and he said your name, quite clearly.'

'Oh, thank God! And is he going to be all right then, Doctor?'

'I think so, Janet. I think so,' Conor answered, with a glance at Anne on the other side of the bed. 'Please God, I think your man's goin' to make it through this.'

Anne put her arms around the woman as another contraction commenced, and Janet's sigh of relief was overtaken by the relentless pain, now dulled a little by the pethidine.

Sister Page went to answer the telephone, and returned with the news that another patient was on her way in, in labour with a third child.

'Her membranes have ruptured, so she'll probably deliver before Mrs Taylor,' she said. 'I'd better prepare the delivery-room for her.'

'Go ahead, Sister, and don't worry,' said Anne. 'I'll stay here and look after Janet.' Turning to Conor, she added, 'You'd better get some rest while you can. You could be called out at any time.'

He was reluctant to leave her sitting up with Janet, and compromised by stretching out in an armchair in the office of Maternity, closing his eyes against the overhead strip-lighting. It was half-past one.

Slowly the night hours passed. Anne dozed for short periods, but Janet's labour made little progress. The other patient arrived and was delivered by Sister Page within an hour. At four o'clock Anne examined Janet's cervix again, and checked another injection of pethidine with Sister Page.

Conor crept into the room where Anne sat in an armchair beside the bed. 'How's she doin'?' he whispered.

Anne shook her head. 'Not much advance, I'm afraid. I think the head's in a posterior position, and it's still well above the pelvic brim. Big baby, too. The membranes are still intact.'

'Good. Foetal heart all right?'

'Yes, I've checked every quarter-hour or so. This could go on for several more hours, and could need helping out when the time comes.' She sighed, suppressing a yawn as she fought with her own fatigue.

They walked down the corridor together, discussing the possible outcome. 'I agree with you, in fact it's exactly what I feel,' muttered Conor with a worried frown. 'This is why I don't like primigravidas in small GP units. I'd really like her to have an epidural—the poor girl needs a break.'

Having no provision for continuous foetal monitoring in the small maternity unit, epidurals could not be used for pain relief at Stretbury. Conor continued to walk slowly up and down the corridor, debating with himself about the problem, and what would be the best course of action for Janet and her child.

'I've come to a decision, Anne,' he said at last. 'We'll transfer her to where she was booked, so that she'll have the facilities of a consultant unit. I'll ring through to the obstetric registar on call, and get on to the ambulance service.'

Anne agreed that this would be the safest course. 'And she'll be under the same roof as her husband,' she added.

'Yes. Intensive Care said he was "stable" when I rang them,' said Conor. 'Apparently the man Palmer's quite poorly, though, with multiple fractures and damage to internal organs—God pity him.' Turning to face Anne, he added, 'The trouble with transferrin' a woman in labour is that a midwife must go with her. Sister Page is free, isn't she?'

'Yes, but I'll go with her,' said Anne. 'Yes, I *will*,' she insisted, overcoming his opposition. 'Seeing that she knows me, and considering the circumstances, it would be better if I stay with her and hand her over to whoever will be caring for her at Bristol.'

The ambulance arrived within fifteen minutes, and Anne summoned up all her willpower and devotion as a nurse to stay alert and cheerful for Janet during the journey, reassuring her and massaging her back during the contractions. It was only after Janet had been admitted to the well-equipped delivery unit under the care of a highly qualified obstetric team that Anne felt her physical and mental powers faltering somewhat; she found herself longing for the presence of Conor McGuire, and the support of his strong arms around her. . .

Giving herself a shake, she got a cup of coffee from a vending machine in the hospital corridor and telephoned from the call-box next to it for a taxi to take her back to Stretbury. She fell asleep on the journey, and it was half-past six when she arrived back in the cool, fresh light of the April morning. Leaving messages for her secretary and Sister Barr that she would not be on duty until eleven unless needed, she wearily climbed the stairs to her flat; after a quick shower she collapsed into her bed, falling asleep immediately.

Hours later there was a tap at her door. She stirred, but did not surface to consciousness until it was repeated.

'Anne! Miss Brittain—may I come in?'

Surely that could not be Dr McGuire in her flat, knocking at the door of her bedroom? Yet it was his voice, without a doubt. Was she dreaming?

'Who is it?' she called out, sitting up. Bright sunshine streamed in between the drawn curtains as the door slowly opened and Conor stood there with two steaming mugs on her little kitchen tray.

'Sure and I just had to come and tell you myself!' he beamed as Anne stared incredulously, clutching the duvet around her. 'I've brewed tea for you, Anne. It's nearly eleven, and your secretary said you were comin' on duty round about now. She was just goin' to phone you, but I was around and told her I'd come up and call you,' he explained. 'You hadn't locked the door of your flat, so I didn't knock—just came in and put the kettle on!'

What on earth must I look like? thought Anne, trying to gather her thoughts together and conscious of her unbrushed hair and crumpled nightie.

He put the tray down on the bedside table, and turned to her with the face of a joyful messenger.

'Oh, Anne, it's grand news that I have for you!'

'Janet!' she cried, remembering everything that had happened and forgetting her looks and the unconventional appearance of a man in her bedroom. 'What news? Has she had the baby? Oh, *tell* me!'

'An eight-pound twelve-ounce boy by Caesarean section twenty minutes ago!' he announced gleefully. 'And Tony's regained consciousness! Yes! They told him in ICU that he'd got a son and he understood—said the baby's name was Andrew—so the paediatrician wrapped up the nipper and took him straight over to ICU from the theatre to show him to his dad, would you believe!'

Anne's wide brown eyes brimmed with tears as she pictured the scene.

'Oh, Conor, how wonderful,' she breathed, clasping her hands together. 'After all they've been through, that dear couple—a little son. . .'

She stopped speaking as she saw the look in his eyes, as blue as an Irish sky in spring, reflecting her own emotion; there was a softness in their depths as he took in her sleep-flushed cheeks and tousled hair, the rather prim white nightie with a frill at the neck. How sweet she was, he thought, and how vulnerable beneath that bossy, self-confident image she cultivated!

'Listen, Anne,' he said, sitting down on the side of the bed. 'Do you have to be around at that man's antenatal clinic this afternoon? Good God, you were up all night, woman!'

'So were you, Conor,' she smiled. 'You didn't know what you were letting yourself in for when you changed with Clive Stepford!'

'No, but I'm glad I was RMO last night, Anne.'

'So am I.' The words were softly uttered, and slipped out before she stopped to think. Hastily recollecting herself, she reached for the mug of tea he had brought her.

'*You* ought to try to get some rest this afternoon, Conor,' she said. 'You're going to the pictures tonight, aren't you?'

'Eh? Oh, so I am, by all the saints!' He laughed and shook his head. 'Sure, I'd completely forgotten about it.'

Elaine won't have forgotten, thought Anne as she drank her tea. He got up and drew back the curtains on another heavenly day.

'Take it easy today, Anne, that's all I'm askin' you,' he said seriously. 'You may be indispensable, but you're still only human.'

He put his mug down on the tray, and before she realised what was happening he bent over her and tenderly kissed her on the forehead.

'You're a darlin',' he whispered as she drew in a sharp breath of surprise.

And then he was out of the door, and she was alone with her confused thoughts and the singing joy in her heart.

Remembering Graham Sellars' joke about locking her bedroom door, and Charles Steynes' warning that she should be careful with McGuire sleeping under the same roof as herself, she laughed softly to herself at the thought of how annoyed she had been with both men! If only they knew about her visitor this morning, whatever would they think?

Yet what was there to remark about it? After all, Conor was a family doctor, and not unfamiliar with bedrooms or their occupants in the course of his daily work; he had even been heard to call his female patients 'darlin' in his teasing Irish way.

But he didn't kiss them as well, did he?

No, but that had been just because of the marvellous news he had come to share with her; it *must* have been, because he was clearly involved with Elaine Lester, wasn't he?

No matter how rational she tried to be, Anne sat up in bed hugging her knees as she remembered the way that he had held her after the ambulance had departed with the crash victims—and the way he had looked at her just now.

And she could not stifle the joy in her heart, no matter how hard she tried. . .

CHAPTER SIX

THE car accident made front-page news in the local paper, and a story also appeared in the *Western Daily Press*. Anne found herself a minor celebrity, with public praise from Lady Hylton and a huge bouquet of spring flowers from Charles Steynes; she used it to make floral arrangements for the entrance hall and staff dining-room. Dr Lester stoped her in the corridor to congratulate her.

'Conor says you were absolutely marvellous, Miss Brittain!' she told Anne rather gushingly. 'Honestly, I can't get him to talk about anything else these days!'

Anne replied politely but a little coolly at being mildly patronised by a woman who clearly wished that *she* had been Conor's assistant that night. Anne's only concern was for the injured men, and she eagerly accepted Conor's suggestion that they should go and visit them in hospital. As they were both free on the Sunday afternoon following the crash, they set off after lunch.

It turned out to be a more extensive round trip than Anne had expected, with both good and grave news as the consequences of the accident became apparent. Tony Taylor had been transferred from Intensive Care to a single room in a male surgical ward; he was quite conscious but suffering from headache and back pain. He had no recollection of the crash, and stared in utter bewilderment at the two strangers at his bedside.

Sensing his feeling of alienation, Anne sat down

beside him and quietly asked him about Janet, who was brought to visit him daily with baby Andrew for him to see and touch.

'I remember my wife being due to have a baby,' he said, 'and now all of a sudden I find that she's had it, and I'm the father of a son—but can't remember anything about his arrival. I feel such an idiot, and I've let Jenny down so badly. I'd promised never to leave her side.'

He winced with a stab of headache, and lay back on his pillows with a gesture of helplessness.

'Please don't be upset, Tony. Jenny understands why you couldn't be there to share the birth. Just think about your lovely son, and give thanks that you've been spared to be his father.' Anne's voice was soft and soothing, and Tony gave her a grateful look.

'Sure, and she's right, Tony. It was no fault o' yours, so don't be reproachin' yourself, friend,' added Conor in the low, gently reassuring tones that Anne remembered from the time of the accident. 'Your Jenny's safely through the birth, and all you've got to do now is rest and let your head mend. Close your eyes and be calm, now. Jenny's happy because you've survived, and so are we all—it's a good man that ye are.'

Tony obediently closed his eyes as they quietly left the room, and Conor went to speak to the staff nurse who was in charge that afternoon. Tony's parents were there, also enquiring about him, and so Conor was able to share the news that they were given: their son was expected to make a good recovery in time, as the EEG and brain-scan results were good. X-rays showed a crack in a vertebra but his spinal cord was undamaged, and his head and back pain would lessen as the local bruising and swelling subsided.

'Your son's made better progress than I ever dared hoped for at the time, and that's a fact,' Conor told the anxious middle-aged couple after introducing himself and Anne. 'Sure, and wouldn't we all be thrown off-course if we got cracked over the skull and couldn't remember a thing about it?'

They nodded uncertainly, wanting to be reassured.

'And congratulations on that lovely grandson of yours,' added Anne, sorry that their distress over their son had cast a shadow over the happy news.

'Yes, we've just come from Maternity,' said Tony's father. 'We're hoping that the baby will give our son an incentive to get better, and we'll do all we can to help Janet.'

'That's great—all the best to you, and keep smilin',' said Conor, holding out his hand to shake each of theirs.

Next they went to Intensive Care to enquire about the other man, John Palmer. When they rang the bell at the entrance to the impressive glass and chromium unit, sited close to the main theatres, a white-overalled nurse answered, and on hearing who they were she invited them to come to the office for an update. On the way there they passed the visitor's waiting room and saw Palmer's son sitting there dejectedly.

'I'll just have a word with the son, if I may,' said Conor suddenly. 'What's his name?'

'Derek,' replied the nurse. 'Dr McGuire—Mr Palmer's condition is very serious. His wife's with him at present, and the son's hoping to go in later, but——' She shrugged meaningly.

Anne followed Conor into the waiting-room, wondering what he would say to the boy, whose eyes

were red and swollen from crying. He recognised them
at once; the very sight of them brought back the nightmare scene after the crash.

'If Dad don't pull through, I don't wanna go on
living,' he said brokenly. 'God, the suspense is driving
me barmy!'

'Courage, son, your mother needs your support,'
said Conor gravely.

'You must be joking, mate—she won't speak to me,
and my brother won't even sit in the same room,'
muttered the youth.

'Oh, he'll come round in time, you'll see. A brother
can't just stop bein' a brother,' replied Conor with a
slight sigh. 'Come now, Derek, show yourself a man.
It's not too late. Your dad——'

'Oh, Dad, Dad, I'll never touch booze again as long
as I live!' groaned Derek, and holding his head
between his hands his self-control gave way and he
shook with despairing sobs. Anne went to sit
beside him.

'All right, Derek, all right. You're sorry and you
never meant to harm your dad,' she murmured, her
arm around his heaving shoulders. 'All you can do now
for him is be brave. Whatever the rest of your family
say, remember they're all worried and upset. Don't
give way to despair, it won't help anybody.' She looked
up helplessly at Conor from above Derek's bowed
head. 'If there was somebody to give him counselling——' she began.

'Perhaps there's a hospital chaplain around somewhere,' he suggested, and when they eventually went
into the ICU office he asked if a priest was available.
The switchboard was contacted and they were told that
a chaplain who had already visited John Palmer would

be up soon to offer what counsel he could to the man's distraught son.

The nurse who had let them into the unit was willing to bend the rules a little with regard to giving information to non-relatives as Conor was the doctor who had first attended Palmer.

'He's had a splenectomy, but there's damage to the liver,' she told them. 'We've transfused twenty pints of blood so far, but his haemoglobin level is still down to single figures. Fractured right clavicle, scapula and humerus, two fractured ribs—and he's developed a pneumothorax since admission.'

'Do you think that——?' began Conor, unwilling to finish the question.

'We don't know, Doctor. He could come through, but the biggest danger now is infection.' She sighed and shook her head.

Through glass partitions Anne could see a bank of electrical equipment monitoring the vital functions of poor John Palmer, who seemed to have tubes and sensors everywhere as he lay under a single sheet for easy nursing access. The temperature and humidity of his room was rigidly controlled, with a constant flow of air. His wife sat beside him, dressed in a white gown and cap, with plastic overshoes on her feet and a surgical mask over her nose and mouth. All these precautions were to prevent organisms from entering the sterile atmosphere surrounding her husband, but to Anne they seemed to exclude all human and emotional contact too.

Their third visit was to the maternity unit where in the postnatal ward they found Janet Taylor, sitting in an armchair with baby Andrew hiccuping in her arms after a feed. It was her fourth day following Caesarean

section and she looked rather tired, but was nevertheless very pleased to see them and talk about Tony.
They enjoyed relaxing and admiring Andrew, trying
to find family resemblances in his chubby features.
Anne asked to cuddle him for a while, unaware that
Conor was observing her intently as she held the baby
and talked delightful nonsense to him while his mother
looked on fondly. When her sister arrived to visit her,
they took their leave.

'Phew! I'm ready for some fresh air and stretchin'
my legs a bit, aren't you?' asked Conor as they walked
back to the car park, thoughtful and subdued after their
three visits. 'D' you fancy an airin' up on the Downs?'

'Wonderful idea!' responded Anne.

'Come on, then, it'll blow the cobwebs away!'

After he had driven up the steep incline of Blackboy
Hill he parked the Fiat by the side of Durdham Down,
and they walked briskly over its curving green expanse
to Clifton Down, taking in the superb view of the Avon
Gorge and the suspension bridge. All around them the
trees were touched with the green mist of tender new
foliage, and above them arched an unclouded blue sky,
paling down towards the west and the Bristol Channel.
A stiff breeze blowing in from the sea ruffled their
hair and reddened their cheeks.

'It certainly *does* blow the cobwebs away!' said
Anne, laughing up into his face exuberantly; he took
her hand and held it as they strode along side by side.

'Anne, you're the best kind o' company to have for
the sort o' visitin' we've done this afternoon,' he told
her with real appreciation. 'You're a sensible woman,
you know what to say to people at a low ebb because
you feel for their trouble with your heart. I'm glad you
came with me, Anne, *mavourneen*!'

Anne had never thought she would be so thrilled at being called 'a sensible woman', but coming from this man it was a compliment that made her eyes sparkle and her cheeks glow even more appealingly. He looked down at her, stopped walking, and drew her towards him. Never a man to hesitate, he flung both arms around her in a bear-hug as they stood among the Sunday strollers, dog-walkers, kite-flyers and children playing on that bright April afternoon. Anne gasped as their cool faces touched, cheek to cheek, and when he moved his head until his lips were upon hers she closed her eyes in momentary rapture, before gently withdrawing herself from him. Resolved though she was not to fall under the spell of Conor's Irish charm, even the briefest of kisses robbed her of rational thought; she gave a shy little laugh as they continued their walk, still holding hands.

'Could you manage a cup of tea, Miss Brittain?' He grinned as they began their descent.

'Gasping,' she replied, thinking how literally true that was, and was happy to race down the hill towards Clifton where they found a little café and squeezed themselves into a cramped table for two. They ordered a pot of tea and toasted currant buns, which arrived piping hot and dripping with melted butter. Anne recovered her breath and tucked in with an appetite sharpened by the fresh air and exercise; she thought that she had never tasted anything so delicious.

'Good God, woman, have you eaten the last bun already? And myself hardly started yet!' exclaimed her companion in mock reproach.

'Oh, have I really?' she apologised. 'Surely there were six, and I've only had two—no, three.' Then, catching sight of the wicked blue gleam in his eye, she

spluttered with indignation. 'You're pulling my leg—
you've eaten just as many! Oh, Conor, you really are
incorrigible!'

'Sure, and it must be your influence on me, Anne.
I'll order another plateful and another pot o' tea!'

'Let me pay half——'

'That you will not. I'm feelin' reckless today. It must
be the spring gettin' to me.'

Their eyes locked across the small table and Anne
saw a tenderness in the cornflower-blue of his gaze
beneath the black brows. He's much too attractive,
she warned herself. No doubt he's like this with every
woman he takes out—Elaine Lester, for instance.
Marshalling her thoughts together, she spoke with
deliberate casualness.

'I meant to ask you, Conor—how did you and Elaine
enjoy the film on Thursday night?'

'Oh, that!' He gave a laugh, but she thought that
he looked a trifle embarrassed. 'Anne, you're a rare
woman for bringin' up awkward subjects, do you know
that? The film was all right, at least I think it was,
seein' that I fell asleep before it was halfway through.'

Anne could not suppress a giggle.

'No, no, it wasn't the fault o' the film, it was myself
needin' my bed after *our* night out on Wednesday,
y'see,' he tried to explain. 'Poor Elaine! Some company I was that evenin'.'

'Well, if you will take your lady-friend to the pictures
when you've been up all the previous night, what can
you expect?' asked Anne with a lofty shrug, though
she could not stifle a tiny satisfaction at the thought
of Elaine turning to him and finding him asleep. 'Hope
you didn't snore,' she added, pouring out another two
cups of tea.

'I should have warned Elaine, but she'd been lookin' forward to seein' the film,' he said, shaking his head wryly. 'Nice girl, Elaine—will make a good GP. Brainy, too. Did you hear she'd won that prize from the drug company—what's it called?—Nutrifare, the one that does all the special dietary products and health foods? They offered a prize for the best essay on the theme o' nutrition, and she got it out of all the entries worldwide.'

'Is that what she wanted to tell you when she came over to the annexe the other morning?' asked Anne, unable to hide her curiosity.

'It was, indeed. She's won a three-week trip to the east coast of the States, all expenses paid, visitin' hospitals and clinics and givin' her essay as a lecture to packed houses,' replied Conor, in what Anne thought was a rather odd manner, as if he was somewhat less than enthusiastic about Elaine's achievement.

'Very nice,' commented Anne. 'When's she taking the trip?'

'Ah, well, now, you see, Anne——' He hesitated.

'Look, don't tell me anything confidential, it's no concern of mine,' said Anne quickly, sensing a certain reluctance on his part.

'It isn't that, Anne, it's just that—Well, Nutrifare is payin' for *two*, y'see, so that Elaine can take a friend—anybody she likes, just as long as they can take three weeks off from their employment, which isn't always so convenient, is it?'

'I see,' murmured Anne. Elaine must have asked Conor to accompany her on this all-expenses-paid trip to the States, and the problem had arisen about two of the GPs being away from the practice for three weeks.

'I don't see why you both can't go, given sufficient

notice,' she said evenly. 'Graham could get a locum in to cover for your absence.'

'Yes, but—Oh, never mind,' he said abruptly, dismissing the subject. 'Listen, Anne, I've had a thought. Seein' that we're here in Bristol, why don't we call on Mrs—er, what's her married name?—Uncle Harry's daughter?'

'Oh, I don't know, Conor,' she said with a frown. 'It's not our job to go chasing patients' relatives who have their own reasons for not visiting. Did you write to her?'

'No, never got round to it, what with the goin's-on this week—but if I were to turn up on her doorstep it might carry more weight than a letter.' He glanced at her unsmiling face. 'I know your views, Anne, but I'd give anything to bring her to see my poor old uncle—it's all he wants in the world. Oh, come on, Anne, don't look like that! Let's go and find her. It's a quarter to six, Sunday teatime. She should be at home.'

'I can't stop you, but I think you're sticking your nose into a situation you don't fully understand,' Anne said doubtfully.

'Good, I knew you'd go along with me,' he said cheerfully, looking up the address in his A to Z of Bristol. 'Here we are—it's in Bedminster.'

When Henry Dodswell's daughter opened the door of the semi-detached council house and saw her visitors she eyed them as suspiciously as her father might have done. A little girl of about six and a boy about two years younger stood on each side of her.

'Miss Brittain!' she said, recognising Anne. 'Why are you—— Oh! Is it my father? He's not——'

'No, no,' said Anne hastily. 'He's——'

'He's missin' you sadly, Sheila,' cut in Conor. 'Good afternoon! My name's Conor McGuire, and I'm your dad's doctor. Would you mind if Miss Brittain and myself have a few words with you?'

Sheila asked them in, and he soon made his message clear to her while the two little children stared at their visitors.

'I'd have to think it over,' said Sheila defensively. 'My father treated me very badly and said he never wanted to set eyes on——'

'Sheila, Sheila, there comes a time when the past has to be put away and forgotten,' said Conor softly. 'The old chap may not have much time left, and you don't want to leave the chance of reconciliation too late.'

'It's all very easy for you to say that!' retorted Sheila. 'You haven't had to put up with his unkindness as I have. He's been wicked to me!'

Her nerves were obviously on edge, and Anne was dismayed at what she saw as Conor's unwarranted interference in other people's lives. She flashed him a warning look, and glanced at the children.

'All right, Sheila, you're under no obligation to visit your father, and I happen to have some idea of how you feel,' she said quietly. 'Why don't you talk it over with your husband, and make up your mind in your own time?'

Sheila blinked back tears in an effort not to break down in front of her children.

'There's been no talking over with my husband since he walked out on us,' she told them stonily. 'And I just couldn't bear that old man to crow over me and say he was right all along. I just *couldn't*——'

Her voice broke on a sob, and Anne closed her eyes involuntarily. Was there any end to other people's troubles this afternoon?

'Sheila, I'm just so sorry to hear that,' she sympathised. 'But I don't think your father would be like that at all. He's changed a lot lately, and there's no doubt that he wants to see you, as Dr McGuire says.' She hesitated, readjusting her standpoint; if Sheila was now on her own, the need to make peace with her father took on a greater importance. 'Look, we'll be on our way now, but we'll leave you with the thought that your father wants you to visit him. It's up to you.'

'And I don't believe that you've an unforgivin' heart,' added Conor. 'Or shall I tell your dad I've had no joy with you?'

'No! Don't say that,' muttered the young mother. 'Tell him I got the message and—and that I'll try to get over one afternoon.'

'Good,' smiled Anne pleasantly. 'And bring these lovely children with you. He'll be so happy to see them—and you.'

'Thanks, Miss Brittain. It was good of you to come all this way.'

'Goodbye, Sheila, and don't be changin' your mind now,' said Conor. 'I wouldn't like you to have regrets for the rest o' your——'

'Goodbye, then, Sheila. We'll look forward to seeing you,' cut in Anne firmly. 'Come along, Dr McGuire, or we'll be late back.'

Sheila stood at the door with the little girl and boy, waving to them as they got into the Fiat.

'I think she'll be over this week,' said Conor.

'Don't say anything to Mr Dodswell in case she doesn't turn up,' cautioned Anne, fastening her seatbelt.

'All right, but I'll lay you a pound to a penny that she does.'

'I never gamble,' said Anne.

The drive back to Stretbury in the clear April evening restored Anne to a sense of peace and tranquillity. She smiled to herself as Conor took the A38 through rolling green farmland in preference to the motorway, and drove for pleasure rather than speed. Anne stole a glance at his profile as he watched the road ahead, a reflective look on his face and a little upward curve on his mouth from time to time, as if quietly enjoying his thoughts. The window was open and a current of air blew across his black hair; Anne thought that he must be the most ruggedly handsome man she had ever met, and her heart beat a little faster as she relived the sensation of those firm lips on her own. In defiance of all her better judgement and resolution, a tremulous happiness flowed through her whole being just sitting beside this man, even the sight of his strong and purposeful hands on the steering-wheel was a reminder of his powerful masculinity and the alarming effect he had on her well-ordered life.

I must watch my step, she told herself for the hundredth time, yet at the same time she closed her eyes and gave herself up to enjoying the evening drive, a journey that she secretly wished could go on and on, travelling beside Conor into the spring night, around the world and beyond. . .

She pulled her thoughts together with a jerk as Sunday's Hill came in sight. 'What a wonderful way to spend a Sunday afternoon!' she said contentedly. 'I'm so glad we went.'

'Sure, and it's great to take time off from work every now and again,' he said, and they both chuckled at the irony of it.

'Anne, could you bear it if I made one more call

before returnin' to base?' he asked. 'A follow-up visit
I ought to have done last week.'

'Honestly, Conor, you just can't keep away from it,
can you?' she smiled, thinking how often this accusation was levelled against herself. 'Who is it?'

'An old guy who had a hernia repair a month ago
and has been rather slow recoverin'. Lost his wife a
couple o' years back, and needs a bit o' cheerin' up.
Name o' Matthew Crawford.'

'Oh, yes, I know him. My mother's his home-help,'
said Anne, recalling her mother's remark about Mr
Crawford liking a drink in bed.

And it was Mrs Brittain who opened the door when
they arrived; her eyes widened at seeing Anne.

'Oh, have I come at an awkward time?' asked
McGuire with a grin. 'I see Matthew has a lady visitor!'

But it was his turn to look surprised when Anne
introduced the lady as her mother, Lilian Brittain,
the home-help he had already met in another
patient's home.

'Heaven protect me, not another o' these indispensable women! I don't think I could cope with *two* o'
you!' he agonised, rolling up his eyes. 'And what have
you been doin' to Matthew, Lilian? Waitin' on him
hand and foot, I'll bet, encouragin' him to be lazy!'
He turned to Mr Crawford. 'Get up out o' that
chair, you old fraud, and stop pretendin' to be an
invalid!'

Matthew got to his feet at once. 'I'm not as young as
I used to be, Doctor,' he protested, a little shamefaced.

'Get away with you, you're only seventy and still in
your prime,' insisted Conor, while Anne and her
mother giggled. 'As long as you avoid liftin' and drag-
gin' heavy weights, you should be leadin' a normal life

by now. In God's name, if I had a charmin' young widow comin' to visit *me*, I'd shift my backside and take her out for an evenin' stroll, so I would!'

Because of McGuire's flow of cheery banter the word 'widow' was not remarked on, though Anne avoided her mother's eye. Matthew took the doctor at his word and went out to the kitchen to start wiping the dishes that Lilian had just finished washing after a shared high tea. Conor was clearly impressed by the kind-hearted housewife, and before he left he paused for a word with her about the other patient in whose home they had met. She blushed with pleasure and smiled her satisfaction at seeing her daughter in the company of the lovely new GP that everybody liked. Anne felt a little embarrassed; she would have to have a chat with her mother to correct any wrong ideas, she decided.

When they arrived back at the hospital and parked behind the Health Centre Conor turned and flung an arm casually around Anne's shoulder.

'It's been a great afternoon, Anne. I've enjoyed havin' your company and meetin' your mother,' he said seriously. 'I hope she's not spoilin' that old man.'

'She's probably spoiling him rotten, but it gives her pleasure—she loves looking after people,' said Anne with a little sigh. 'He's not the only client who gets extra unpaid visits from her.'

'Really? You've taken after her, then, Anne.'

There was a pause during which Anne could think of nothing to say. He touched her cheek with his forefinger, gently stroking it down the side of her face until it was under her chin. He lifted her face to his, so that she had to look into those dark, unfathomable blue pools.

'Women like you and your mother are the salt of the earth,' he said simply.

Anne tried to warn herself that she had no wish for endearments from a man who was involved with another woman.

'Oh, no, Conor, I——'

But his kiss on her lips stilled any protest she had been about to make, and the delirious sensation momentarily blotted out all other thoughts. When he drew away from her she had no words, but her response was there for him to read in the dark depths of her startled brown eyes.

But not for long. She quickly got out of the car, and looked around to check that there had been no spectators.

'Goodnight, Conor. And thank you.'

'Goodnight, Anne. And thank you, too.'

If he whispered anything else she did not hear it as she turned and walked towards the hospital entrance, her wildly pounding heart at war with her common sense and caution.

Anne normally took Monday afternoons off to do a little shopping in Stretbury, but on this particular Monday she decided to attend to the two large hanging baskets that she put up on each side of the hospital front entrance every spring. Dressed in jeans and a 'Save the Children' sweatshirt, she assembled the bag of compost and the stepladder from the garden shed behind the building, and set to work with the seedlings she had bought at a garden centre on Saturday. Absorbed in her task, she was quite oblivious to the tall figure who stood silently admiring her back view as she transferred the little green plants from their plastic trays to the rich, dark compost she had pressed down into the baskets.

A man's commanding tone broke in on her thoughts.

'I say—you there—gardener's boy! Can you tell me where I might find the Senior Nursin' Administrator o' this hospital?'

Anne spun round to face the questioner, and her eyes sparkled mischievously as she put on the blankest of expressions.

'Aah, she bain't around this afternoon, gaffer. She be gone fur to make a complaint against one o' them doctors, loike,' she replied in a broad Gloucestershire burr.

Conor grinned, but quickly assumed a worried look. 'Is that so, boy? Which one o' the doctors is she out to destroy?'

'Aah, 'e be that cracked Irish feller, Oi tell ee! 'E be neither use nor ornament, sez she.'

'Heaven save the man from the old battle-axe! Will you tell her from me that—No! *Don't*!' He backed away as Anne advanced towards him with the watering-can, its long spout dripping ominously. 'It's jokin' that I was, just jokin'!'

Anne laughed and returned to her task. 'You're just in time to help me hang these up. Can you hold the stepladder?'

'No, you hold it and I'll put them up,' he said firmly.

Moving the ladder and disputing between themselves about where best to place it, neither of them noticed the woman with two small children who had got off the bus near the entrance to the drive. They walked up to where Anne and Conor were putting up the second basket.

'Er—excuse me, but where can I find——? Oh, Miss

Brittain!' said Sheila in surprise at seeing the somewhat
grubby figure holding the ladder, which rocked a little
as Conor came down the steps.

'*Sheila*! You've come!' they cried out in unison, and
Conor made a face at Anne. 'Told you she would,' he
whispered, and then firmly grasped Sheila's arm.
'Come with me!'

Anne wiped her hands quickly and followed with
the children, a trusting little hand in each of hers as
they took the garden path to the Hylton Annexe
where the residents were having their tea on the
veranda. Henry was not among them, for which Anne
was glad, it would be better for the meeting to take
place in the privacy of his room.

Sister Mason saw them coming and welcomed Sheila
at the door.

'I'm so glad you've come, dear,' she smiled, and
went ahead of them to Henry's room. The door was
closed, and there was no answer to her knock.

'Mr Dodswell! Henry!' she called, opening the door
and putting her head round it. He was sitting at the
window, looking out at the garden in just the same
morose way as when Anne had first taken Conor to
see his 'uncle'. An untouched tray of tea was on the
table beside him.

'There's a visitor for you, Henry,' said the sister.

'Ah, Conor, he's a good 'un,' sighed the old man.
'He did his best, but I know what he's come to tell
me. She doesn't want anything to do with me, and I'm
not surprised.'

Conor put a finger to his lips and went into the
room alone.

'Sure and it's myself, Uncle Harry, come to cheer
you up!'

The old man forced a smile. 'You're good to a miserable old bugger like me, Conor.'

'Thanks, Uncle. And I've got a surprise for you today,' said Conor softly, his eyes resting on Henry with real affection. 'Look here!'

He beckoned to Sheila, and Henry saw her; his mouth dropped open, but at once the light came back into his eyes.

'Hello, Dad,' she said. 'It's good to see you again.'

'Sheila—my girl, my little girl——' quavered the old man, stretching out his arms towards her. 'Oh, my little girl. . .' His words trailed off into a sob.

Conor glanced towards Anne and saw that her eyes were misty as the father and daughter embraced and two bewildered children found themselves hugged by an old gentleman with tears running down his leathery cheeks. Anne returned Conor's look, and by unspoken agreement she gently led the little girl and boy away from the emotional scene until Henry and Sheila had calmed a little. She took them into the kitchen of the annexe and found some orange juice and biscuits for them. Conor followed them in triumph.

'We've done it, Anne, we've done it!' he declared in delight. 'And I know just the lady who'll want to meet Sheila's children!'

Anne looked up with a radiant smile. 'Of course—Miss Knight, who else? Oh, Conor, you were right!'

He leaned towards her and kissed the tip of her nose.

'Remember that when I'm next in your bad books, Anne, *mavourneen*. Can I have a biscuit, too?'

CHAPTER SEVEN

THE spring days passed quickly, and Anne was kept so busy that she scarcely noticed when April gave place to May. A couple of weeks of showery weather gave way to a blaze of sunshine, revealing the awakened earth in all its verdant beauty. Drifts of hawthorn blossom lay on the hedgerows like flowering snow, and in the meadows around Stretbury new baby calves grazed beside their mothers in the black and white dairy herds.

Lady Margaret Hylton was holding a meeting over coffee one morning in the boardroom, to discuss plans for the summer fête in July. Anne had asked the ward sisters to attend, and Marjorie Stepford, now seven months pregnant, also put in an appearance with Mrs Sellars.

When the arrangements for the fête had been made Lady Hylton was eager to catch up on hospital gossip, and asked if it was true that Dr McGuire was to accompany Dr Lester on her prize trip to the States. Nobody seemed to know for certain, and Anne murmured vaguely about there being some difficulty with two GPs being absent from the practice for the same three-week period.

'Nonsense! Graham can easily get a couple of locums in,' Lady Hylton affirmed. 'There must be lots of newly qualified doctors who would simply *love* to come to a place like Stretbury!' A gleam of interest lit her features. 'Tell me, is there a special understanding between those two?'

123

There was a pause while smiles and knowing glances passed between some of the hospital staff.

'They're certainly together a lot, and often go for their lunch at the Huntsman,' said Sister Louise Barr in an amused tone. 'She's always chatting about some film that they've seen, and I know she's very keen on taking him to the USA on this trip.'

'How very nice! And so suitable,' beamed Margaret Hylton indulgently. 'With so much in common, and both of them such popular doctors, it would be an excellent match. Still, perhaps we mustn't jump to conclusions too soon.'

'Conor McGuire isn't popular with *everybody*, Lady Hylton,' drawled Louise Barr slyly. 'We know a certain consultant surgeon who can't stand the sight of him—don't we, Miss Brittain?'

Anne flushed angrily. 'If you mean Mr Steynes, I can assure you that he has settled down very well with Dr McGuire as his regular anaesthetist,' she said firmly. 'It really isn't that uncommon for doctors to clash when they have to work together in a tense situation and haven't had time to get to know each other's ways.'

'That's true, but I must admit that I'd heard the same about them,' remarked Marjorie Stepford. 'Two such very different personalities are bound to have difficulties at first, aren't they?'

Catching Anne's eye, Lady Hylton tactfully steered the conversation towards other topics.

'How's the dear little Taylor baby?' she enquired.

'Andrew? Oh, he's gorgeous!' enthused Anne. 'Five weeks old, and I'm told he's smiling at his daddy already. Of course Tony's home now, and Janet doesn't have that journey every day to visit him.'

'He's made a very good recovery, I understand?'

'Pretty good, yes, though he still gets headaches and tires easily,' answered Anne with caution. 'He has to go to Bristol for neurological checks, and has had another CAT scan of his head. They're reasonably happy about him—he's done better than we ever dared to hope.'

'Thanks to the wonderful work done by you and Dr McGuire,' said Margaret Hylton smilingly, with embarrassing insistence on the part played by her 'first-aiders', as she called them. 'I've been told that the other man is gradually pulling through, too.'

Anne hesitated. 'He's still quite poorly in hospital, and may not be able to work again.' She sighed. 'His son Derek visits him every day, and helps with the physiotherapy. Tha boy has learned a terrible lesson and is a changed character, by all accounts.'

Lady Hylton nodded grave approval. 'So some good may have come out of the whole ghastly business, then.'

There were head-shakings round the table, and Lady Hylton introduced a new topic.

'Are there any vacancies at present in the Hylton Annexe?' she asked.

'We always try to keep one bed empty for an emergency admission, Lady Hylton, and that's all we've got at present,' replied Anne. 'Though I think there could be another vacancy in a week or two.'

'Oh, dear! I suppose you mean that you are expecting a—a departure?' murmured Margaret with a nod.

'Well, no, not in the way you're thinking,' smiled Anne. 'Our Mr Dodswell has been going out at weekends to stay with his daughter and grandchildren in Bedminster, and I wouldn't be at all surprised if he moves out of the annexe to live with them permanently.'

'Dodswell? Do you mean that perfectly dreadful old man who was so rude to me at Christmas?' asked Lady Margaret incredulously. 'Don't tell me he's had a change of heart so late in life!'

'As a matter of fact, he *has*, I'm happy to say,' Anne informed her. 'He's a different man now that he's been reconciled with his daughter, and it's been Dr McGuire's doing. He took on Henry as a surrogate uncle, and went to a lot of trouble to heal the rift—and succeeded.'

'Wonderful! And so we're back to the Irish boy again! He just won't stay out of the conversation, will he?' smiled the good-humoured lady, who then went on to speak of her plans for making Stretbury Memorial into an NHS Trust hospital, with Graham Sellars and Anne Brittain as managers, assisted by her own accountants. Anne smiled to herself; the lady clearly intended to keep her friends in positions of authority, thus preserving her own unofficial control of the hospital that she still considerd hers. Anne was sure that it could fall into worse hands than the benevolent JP's, and gave her discreet approval of the plans.

The meeting broke up in an atmosphere of goodwill, and Anne looked forward to a long-awaited afternoon off. It was high time to invest in that new look for her wardrobe, she decided, and set off in her car to Bristol for a shopping spree.

It was a bright, sunny afternoon, and after leaving the car in a multi-storey car park near to the Broadmead shopping centre she mingled with the crowds and stared into an endless variety of windows full of spring fashions. Choosing the right clothes was more difficult than she had anticipated; wandering around Marks and Spencer, looking at any number of possible outfits, she was struck by the thought that a good friend with a flair for clothes would make the business of choosing a whole lot easier. Anne reflected that she could not think of any such intimate friends of her own age; the former nursing friends with whom she had trained were now scattered, some married, and most living at a distance. She was on good terms with her staff, but the work that meant so much to her tended to set her apart from the kind of feminine intimacies that most women enjoyed, and she felt a little wistful that there seemed to be nobody she could call upon to help her choose new clothes and accessories for the spring.

She went to take a look at some smaller dress shops, and it was in a select little boutique that she ran into Elaine Lester, trying on a hat.

'Miss Brittain! How nice to see you,' said the young doctor pleasantly. 'Look, can I ask you a favour? Please help me to decide between these two hats! Should I have the straw one with the wide, romantic brim? Or this dear little tricorn with flowers sprouting from the back?'

Anne laughed. 'Impossible to decide! They both look super on you, Dr Lester. Two hats for two different moods. Can't you have them both?'

'I can't really afford it, but I will. Thank you! And if a certain person accuses me of extravagance, I shall blame *you*, Miss Brittain,' replied Elaine happily, getting out her chequebook. 'Right, I'll take them both.'

'Are you in a hurry?' asked Anne as an idea suddenly flashed into her head.

'No, just wandering around to get some ideas for my trip to the States. Why, did you want to have a word about something, Miss Brittain?' asked Elaine rather warily, knowing of the administrator's tendency to talk shop when off duty.

'I just wondered if we could help each other choose some clothes, that's all,' ventured Anne. 'I need a couple of new outfits, you see, and I really could do with an adviser to stop me buying anything wildly unsuitable!'

'It would be a pleasure,' said Elaine at once. 'Two heads are better than one, they say! Come on, let's do our shopping together, Miss Brittain.'

'Oh, do call me Anne—and thanks a lot, Elaine.'

For the next two hours they toured the shops, trying on dresses, blouses, skirts and jackets; one would parade in front of the other, considering and criticising. By four o'clock both felt that they had had a successful afternoon, and Anne was the owner of a charming dress in flowered silk with a blue background that softly flattered her slim figure. She had also bought a mix-and-match medley consisting of a skirt, trousers, jacket, vest top and long shirt that could combine to make a whole variety of different outfits. She was delighted, even excited with her purchases, and stopped to buy one more item as they left Marks and Spencer and some glamorous swimwear caught her eye.

'A new swimsuit, that's what I need!' she said, and, having almost decided on a boldly patterned model, she was persuaded by Elaine to go for a plain navy one-piece suit with a white diagonal flash. It had a low back and moulded bra front, and Anne imagined herself wearing it at the new swimming baths in the recently opened leisure centre in Stretbury.

'And now, Elaine, the next thing on our agenda is *tea*, a proper high tea, and it's my treat,' she insisted. 'There's a nice place that my mother likes, tucked away in a little street just off the centre.'

They made their way to the tea-shop and took a seat. Anne passed the menu to Elaine and asked her to choose something nice. Salads and scones were brought to their table, and Anne poured out two cups of tea.

'Tell me more about the Nutrifare prize and your trip to the USA,' she invited.

'Oh, Anne, it's so exciting,' sighed the young doctor, her eyes shining as she outlined the proposed itinerary for the three weeks abroad while Anne listened indulgently.

'Conor's not too happy about two of us being a[way] from the practice, but I'm willing to wait as long [as it] takes to sort out a locum—or two locums,' enthus[ed] Elaine. 'Oh, Anne, isn't he the most amazing man? So original and go-ahead in his attitude to positive health. I mean, he doesn't just treat the symptoms of a condition, he treats the whole person, and the situation that they are in.'

'I know what you mean,' agreed Anne, though her heart sank a little at the prospect of listening to this eulogy of Conor's holistic approach to medicine all through the meal. It was disconcerting to be faced with a woman so obviously in love with a man who also stirred forbidden emotions in herself. She would have to be very careful in her responses, she thought.

'I never dreamed that when I came to Stretbury as a junior partner in a rural practice I'd meet a man like Conor McGuire, Anne,' went on the rapturous Elaine. 'And he's so *nice* with it, so willing to discuss a case history with me, or to take me out to a film or a show that he knows I'd like to see. And he's no respecter of status, is he? I mean, nursing auxiliaries and home-helps all adore him because he treats them in just the same way as his medical colleagues. It's his niceness to everybody he meets——'

Anne wondered if Elaine had yet encountered the infuriatingly stubborn streak in her idol. She also won-dered if Elaine had read anything more into Conor's 'niceness to everybody' than was justified, regarding his feelings towards her personally. Deep down in her secret heart Anne questioned whether a man truly in love with one woman would behave so lovingly on occasion towards another—herself—in the way that he had done, but perhaps *she* was now reading too much into those softly spoken endearments, those elec-trifying kisses that had so moved her own heart. They probably meant much less to him, she thought, with a little shrug of self-mockery.

Meanwhile Elaine continued to chatter confidingly over the tea, and Anne listened patiently until all of a sudden she saw something behind Elaine's shoulder that made her stare in shocked surprise. Elaine noticed her change of expression, and was about to turn round to see the cause of it.

'No! Don't look now, Elaine,' begged Anne in a whisper. 'Wait until they've sat down at a table.'

'*Who*? What is it?' asked her companion, alarmed by Anne's urgent tone

'Elaine, it's the man himself—Conor, I mean—and he's with a woman,' murmured Anne. 'They're just sitting down. He's got his back to us, she's facing me.'

Elaine at once turned round, ignoring Anne's warn-ing. Conor's broad shoulders and black hair were unmistakable, and his companion, a willowy, dark-haired woman of around forty, had large, striking, mournful eyes and a pretty red mouth. She was gazing at him intently, listening eagerly to every word he was saying to her; they seemed to have eyes only for each other.

Elaine turned back to face Anne; she was pale and trembling, wanting nothing more to eat.

'Elaine, she could be *anybody*,' began Anne, having to hide her own dismay at this proof of Conor's closer acquaintance with women other than themselves. 'A relative, maybe, or a patient's relative——'

At that moment Conor turned to catch the waitress's eye, and instead he caught Anne's. For an instant they stared straight at each other in mute recognition, and he also saw Elaine. He gave Anne the briefest of nods and a half-smile of acknowledgement, then turned away and spoke in a low voice to his woman-friend. Anne saw her dark eyes widen, and he placed his hand over hers on the table.

Anne felt truly sorry for Elaine, who had noticed this brief exchange of looks, and was raising her teacup with a hand that shook. McGuire could not have made his wishes more clear: he did not want to be disturbed, nor did he wish to introduce them to the lady.

'Another cup of tea, Elaine?' asked Anne gently. 'Then I'll ask for the bill and we'll be on our way, shall we?'

Elaine looked at her levelly across the table.

'What an utter fool you must think me,' she said.

'Of course I don't. And I shan't mention a word of this to a soul,' Anne assured her, forcing a smile and hiding her own sense of shock.

Elaine continued as if Anne had not spoken. 'But

I'm not quite such a fool, you see,' she said stonily.
'I know perfectly well why a man takes a woman out
and doesn't want to be seen by anybody he knows.
It's because one or both of them are married, and
they're having an illicit affair. From the quick look I
had of her, she seems just the type,' she added, with
a hard little mirthless laugh.

'Now, Elaine, don't jump to conclusions,' remon-
strated Anne, though this had been her own first
suspicion. 'We don't *know* that. There's probably a
perfectly simple explanation why he doesn't want to
know us this afternoon.'

'Yes, and I've just given it,' replied the young
woman bluntly. 'Oh, come on, Anne, let's go. I don't
care for being cold-shouldered by someone I thought
was——'

She bit her lip, and Anne quickly rose to pay the
bill and escort her out of the tea-shop. While sympath-
ising with the humiliation that Elaine felt Anne still
had her own whirling emotions to control, and realised
that she was trembling.

And what exactly did she feel? she asked herself as
she drove back to Stretbury, having seen Elaine into
her own car and made her promise to drive carefully.
Meeting Conor with a woman-friend had been an
unpleasant surprise to her also, and Elaine's specu-
lation about an illicit liaison might well be correct.
Anne sighed as she thought of Elaine driving back
alone, fighting her tears of jealously and disappointment. So much for the knowing remarks of Louise
Barr and other hospital staff! Elaine had made her
feelings for McGuire all too evident to everybody she
knew, and would now have to face the questioning
looks, the sympathy or amusement of her acquaint-

ances. Anne, on the other hand, had kept her feelings for the same man completely hidden from everybody except possibly himself, so would not now have to endure the same humiliation as Elaine. Nevertheless she felt the same heartache, the bewilderment, the sense of being shut out of an important part of the life of this man; all this was as bitter to her as to the young woman doctor.

Only. . . Anne still felt somehow that she had a truer perception of McGuire's character than Elaine had, and she could not believe him to be the kind of man who would carry on a clandestine relationship with another man's wife, however much the circumstantial evidence seemed to point to it. Anne had seen a deep unhappiness in the eyes of the woman with him, almost a haggard look upon a face that should have been beautiful; there was tragedy somewhere in the situation, and almost to her own surprise Anne found herself hoping that somehow, some way, Conor McGuire might be able to bring a little hope and comfort to a sorrowing heart.

After putting away her purchases Anne felt distinctly at a loose end. She had looked forward to her half-day, but now even her pretty new clothes failed to raise her spirits. She thought of calling on her mother, but knew that Matthew Crawford would be at the bungalow, helping Lilian to redecorate the kitchen in washable vinyl wall-covering, with ceramic tiles around the sink unit. During the past few weeks the former patient had improved in his general health and mental vigour, and Anne suspected that he felt more than just gratitude towards his home-help. If so, he would have to be disillusioned, she thought grimly, for Lilian Brittain was not divorced and had no idea of the whereabouts of her errant husband. Anne's dark eyes took on an unfamiliar hardness as she considered her mother's ambiguous position: no husband to care for her and no freedom to accept the love and protection of any other man. It was so unfair! On her part, Anne had no desire to intrude upon the easygoing comradeship between Lilian and Matthew—there was no harm in it, and she hoped that they were enjoying their decorating, no doubt punctuated by tasty snacks and welcome cups of tea.

Meanwhile she had to come to terms with a heavenly May evening and nobody with whom to share it; a melancholy mood descended on her as she contemplated the prospect. She knew that she had to put Conor McGuire out of her mind once and for all, and make more effort to cultivate interests and activities outside her work. But *how*, when her irregular working hours prevented her from joining a tennis or swimming-club on a regular basis? Any kind of evening class would so often have to be missed because of being on duty, and an amateur dramatic society was out of the question; she simply would not be able to commit herself to attending rehearsals. Anne had always been aware of these disadvantages, but never before had she felt so keenly her lack of a social life and a circle of intimate friends. She gave a little shiver in spite of the warmth of the evening, and for the first time in her life admitted to herself that she was lonely.

What should she do? Anne braced her shoulders and made her way towards the place where she knew she would always be welcomed: the Hylton Annexe. As a dedicated nurse she knew that her patients were always comforting, and the long-term elderly residents were especially so. Yes! There was no doubt about it, the annexe was the best cure for self-pity that she could think of.

Anne settled down beside Miss Knight in her padded chair on the veranda. The old lady's general condition had improved enormously, and she had put on nearly two stone in weight. She was much more mobile, venturing out into the grounds with a jaunty step, the faithful Tabitha never far away. She no longer spent her afternoons dozing, but had taken up crocheting knee-blankets for the residents, and read the quality newspapers to keep herself well-informed. She had become a confidante and spokeswoman for the less articulate residents, and Anne always appreciated her insight. A real bond had developed between the old teacher and her one-time pupil, and although Anne could not tell Miss Knight about the afternoon's encounter in the tea-shop she was soon deep in conversation about the television dramatisation of a classic novel that everybody was watching, including Miss Knight. So absorbed was Anne in this shared critical appraisal that she did not notice the arrival of the well-built man who came and sat down in the chair on the other side of her.

'Good evening, Sister Anne. They told me I'd find you here.'

Anne turned round in amazement.

'Mr Steynes! Whatever are you doing at Stretbury at this hour?' she asked. 'Oh, by the way, this is my friend Miss Victoria Knight.'

'Good evening, Miss Knight. I've heard Anne speak of you,' he said with a ready smile, reaching across Anne to shake the old lady's hand. 'I happened to be on my way back from seeing a couple of private

patients near Gloucester and thought I'd drop off to
see Marjorie Stepford. And then I thought to myself,
I believe Sister Anne's off duty, and might offer me
some tea—or is that being too presumptuous?'

His smile was so charming and his manner so friendly
that Anne could only smile and offer to brew a pot of
tea in the kitchen of the annexe.

'We'll make it tea for the three of us,' she said.

'My dear Anne, you're much too kind—it's quite
unpardonable of me to impose on you and Miss Knight
like this,' he apologised. 'Just wait a minute, though,
I might have an even better idea.' He glanced at his
watch. 'Suppose I were to ask you two delightful ladies
to come out to supper with me? There's a rather nice
little place in Wotton—or would Miss Knight prefer
the Huntsman?'

Anne was quite taken aback by this totally unexpected invitation, and her first thought was to decline
politely on behalf of them both. But then she had
second thoughts as she realised what a treat this would
be for Victoria—to go for a drive on a lovely May
evening and stop for supper at a nice restaurant in the
company of an attentive host and mutual woman-
friend—herself. How could anybody object? Anne had
enough self-awareness to admit that it would be
pleasant for her, too, after the gloomy thoughts she'd
had earlier. It really was most kind of Mr Steynes, and
no doubt a diversion for him as well, poor man, stuck
with that alcoholic wife and no proper family life to
go home to! Yes, she would accept; she could think
of no earthly reason why she should not.

'How do you feel about it, Miss Knight?' she asked
encouragingly. 'Shall we seize the opportunity and go
for a little run?'

'Well, if Mr Steynes is sure, and you feel that it would be all right for me to go, Anne dear——'

'Nothing would give me greater pleasure, Miss Knight,' beamed Steynes, and so it was settled.

Anne went to tell Winnie Mason that she was taking Victoria out, and she suddenly remembered how McGuire had taken old Henry Dodswell down to the pub on the evening of her very first meeting with him. Damn the man, she thought crossly, though his idea had turned out to be a good one—as would this little outing for Victoria.

Sister Mason said that she would help the old lady to get ready, with a lightweight jacket over her dress and a change of shoes.

'I expect you'll want to pop up to your flat, Miss Brittain,' she suggested tactfully. 'And then you can collect Victoria in about a quarter of an hour, shall we say?'

Anne was glad of an opportunity to put on her new silk dress and renew her make-up. When she came down the stairs Charles Steynes was waiting for her in the entrance-hall.

'Ah, there you are, Anne, my dear, how perfectly lovely you look! I've been thinking, and I know *just* the place for us—a nice, secluded little cottage where all the cooking is done by the couple who run it. It will be just right, I'm sure!'

His rather booming tones could be heard for some distance, and Anne caught her breath as she saw McGuire coming in at the front door and passing behind Steynes to go down the corridor to the Health Centre for his evening surgery. Just for one moment he looked up and caught her eye as she stood on the stairs. Steynes was also looking up at her in undisguised admiration, and Anne stared wide-eyed at both men until McGuire turned his head sharply away and strode furiously towards the centre, not having uttered a word.

Had he heard what Steynes had said? Anne felt suddenly defiant. Why on earth should she feel the need to explain to Conor McGuire that Miss Knight was to join them? Good heavens, she thought, it's all right for *him* to take some mysterious woman out to tea and ignore me and poor Dr Lester when we run into them by accident! I don't have to apologise to him for anything!

The evening excursion turned out to be quite pleasant. Charles Steynes was consideration itself, helping Miss Knight by offering his arm, finding a comfortable chair for her and generally attending to her every need. Anne saw how much her old teacher was enjoying the change from daily routine, and could only feel grateful to Steynes for his kindness.

On arriving back at the hospital, soon after eight, Anne politely declined Charles's invitation to go for a drink with him after leaving Miss Knight at the annexe. She said that she would see Victoria tucked up in bed as the old lady looked tired after the excitement of the outing. So, thanking him again, she waved goodbye as he drove off towards Bristol.

When Victoria was settled in her bed Anne prepared a warm drink of malted milk for her, and sat down at the bedside.

'Did you enjoy it, Miss Knight?' she asked softly.

'Yes, Anne dear, I did,' said the old lady with a smile. 'And did you enjoy it, too, Anne?'

'Why, of course I did, Miss Knight! Who would not? It was a good idea of Mr Steynes', and quite unexpected,' replied Anne, smiling back at her.

'He is in love with you, Anne. You do know that, don't you?'

Anne was too astonished to do anything but stare back at her old teacher in disbelief. Miss Knight had the same unfounded suspicions as Conor!

'Ah, I see that you're surprised, Anne,' said the old lady with a sigh. 'Perhaps an outsider sees things more clearly sometimes. Charles Steynes is one of those men who would go to great lengths to get what he wants— even to taking an old woman out as a chaperon! But a woman with your beliefs and principles would never find happiness with a man who is committed elsewhere, and I'm sure you know that.'

She paused and looked towards the window where the light was beginning to fade. Anne continued to sit absolutely still, too stunned by what she had just heard to make any reply. If it had been anybody else but Miss Knight saying such things to her. . .

'What *does* worry me, Anne, is that you could suffer tremendous pain if he succeeded in leading you into an entanglement,' the quiet old voice continued. 'Believe me, dear, I know from my own experience what temptations there can be for the lonely single woman. You are worth something better than that, Anne. You *deserve* better. And, if I'm not mistaken, you will not have to look very far for it.'

She stopped speaking, and lay back on her pillow. There was complete silence in the room for some minutes. At length Anne rose from her chair and drew the curtains.

'I really don't know quite what to say, Miss Knight.'

'You don't have to say anything, Anne. Just think about it, that's all. Goodnight.'

'Goodnight—Victoria.'

And, feeling like a little girl at school once again, leaving the headmistress's study, Anne Brittain walked out of the annexe and thoughtfully made her way back to the main building.

She had put Conor's dislike of Steynes down to a personality clash between two men with strong characters but very different ideas—but Victoria Knight had no reason to criticise a man who had shown her kindness and generosity in the way that Mr Steynes had done today.

Unless. . . Anne frowned. Miss Knight had always shown a keen perception of character, ever since Anne had known her. It was a disturbing thought that Anne could not shake off.

CHAPTER EIGHT

IT WAS two days later when Anne went into the staff dining-room at lunchtime, and saw Elaine Lester sitting alone at a table and reading a newspaper.

'Mind if I join you?' Anne asked, and Elaine smiled briefly, indicating the chair opposite. Anne noticed that the doctor had not much colour but seemed composed enough, though she had lost the flow of girlish chatter which had sometimes made her a little irritating in the past. Like me, she's thrown herself into her work as a cure for personal heartache, thought Anne, always pleased to see a woman pick herself up after a disappointment in love. She smiled and remarked on the postcards they had all received from Dr and Mrs Sellars, on holiday in the Algarve.

'I'll send you some pictures of the places I visit on the eastern seaboard,' said Elaine. 'The trip's fixed for late September, so I shall be just at the right time for the "fall" which is supposed to be so spectacular—all those blazing reds and yellows in Vermont!'

'Oh, so you've got a date for departure, then?' said Anne. 'Something to look forward to—that's nice.'

'Yes, it certainly is. By the way, I've asked my friend Julia from medical school days to share the trip with me, Anne,' she added quickly, looking down at her plate as she spoke. 'Honestly, she's so thrilled—simply can't wait to board the plane!'

'Oh, *good*!' answered Anne with genuine pleasure. 'I'm just so glad that you've managed to—er——'

'Find a replacement? Yes, no problem. Dr McGuire never really wanted to go, of course, I can see that now. It was my idea entirely, and he must have felt so embarrassed. I know why now, don't I? Silly me! Never mind, we all know where we stand now, and I'm not one for looking back.'

'Good for you,' nodded Anne, wondering what Elaine would say if she knew how hard Anne was finding it to get the same man out of *her* system.

On the following Thursday, the day of the antenatal clinic, Charles Steynes drove over to Stretbury well before it was due to start. He found Anne preparing for the clinic session with Sister Wendy Garrett.

'Good afternoon, ladies,' he smiled. 'I'm a little early today, so is there any chance of coffee? If your office is available, Sister Anne, I'd be glad of a quiet word.'

Anne hesitated, just for a moment; Miss Knight's words had stayed with her, even though she considered the old lady mistaken for once.

'All right, Mr Steynes, though I haven't much time to spare,' she replied, thinking that her secretary would probably be on her lunch-break. She set aside the sheaves of case-notes she had been sorting while Wendy Garrett tactfully continued setting out examination gloves and paper sheets.

'You look rather tired today, my dear, and where are the roses in your cheeks? Are you keeping well, Anne?' asked Steynes with an air of concern as they went into her office and he closed the door.

'Yes, thank you, Mr Steynes. It's been a busy time.' She shrugged as she filled the electric coffee-percolator.

'What a treasure you are,' he murmured, his eyes

fixed on her as she set out two cups on a tray.

'I beg your pardon, Mr Steynes?' she said, looking up sharply at his changed tone of voice. 'What exactly did you want to discuss with me?'

'Oh, Anne, you're a woman in a thousand!' he breathed. 'But of course I've known that for a long time, haven't I? You've been such a wonderfully understanding friend to me!'

'I appreciate your kindness the other evening, Mr Steynes——' she began, now thoroughly alerted by the look in his eyes—the unmistakable gleam of desire. Could McGuire and Miss Knight really have been right all along?

'Ah, I'd like to do so much for you, Anne!' He took a step towards her and, before she realised what was happening, his arms were round her and his lips were pressed firmly on her mouth. She recoiled in shocked surprise from his hot breath, from his hoarsely whispered, 'Darling!'

'Mr Steynes! What are you thinking of? Let me go at once!' she gasped, attempting to free herself from the grip of his arms. She was soon seriously struggling, for Steynes was a strong, burly man with powerful muscles, and she was no physical match for him.

'Don't pretend any longer, little Anne—I've seen the way you've looked at me in the theatre!' he muttered, aroused even further by what he saw as a show of resistance. 'It's high time we both started being honest with each other——'

Anne wrenched her mouth away from his and gave a scream; there was a thud as she kicked over a chair in her efforts to break free of his hold on her. Steynes remembered that the door was not locked, and when the sound of rapid footsteps was heard he swore under his breath and pushed Anne away, none too gently, just as the door was pulled open and Conor McGuire appeared on the threshold.

The couple presented an almost comical picture. Anne stood panting and flushed, her hair dishevelled and her uniform belt pulled round her waist so that the silver buckle was at the side instead of the front. Steynes' hair flopped over his forehead, and his unloosened tie dangled outside his jacket. His face was almost purple with vexation and he glared malevolently at the intruder.

'*Conor*!' breathed Anne.

McGuire completely ignored her, and flashed Steynes a look of utter contempt.

'Sure, I always thought yer a lecher, but I didn't think yer'd sink this low,' he growled with dangerous calm. 'Get out.'

'Now look here, McGuire, I've had enough of your bloody Irish——' blustered Steynes, but McGuire cut in peremptorily.

'Yer heard what I said. *Out*.'

'For God's sake, Mr Steynes, do as he says!' hissed Anne in genuine fear of what McGuire might do.

Steynes turned an incriminating eye on her. 'Don't try to offload all the blame on to *me*, Anne,' he threatened. 'You know perfectly well why you asked me to come in here with you!'

He had intended to make a nonchalant exit from the office, but when McGuire heard this accusation of Anne his self-control gave way, and he threw a furious punch that landed on Steynes' fleshy jaw. The surgeon staggered backwards with blood spurting from a cut lip; he fell against the desk, but quickly felt for the edge of it to steady himself, and stood breathing heavily as he eyed McGuire, who was making a visible effort to control himself. Anne looked on with bated breath, and at last McGuire turned his head towards her and spoke in a voice like dry ice.

'I warned ye about this louse, but ye took no heed o' me. How a woman o' sense could be so blind, the devil only knows. And himself wid the nice wife and all—thinks the world o' him, she does, the poor darlin'—thinks she's let him down. Hah!' McGuire almost spat. 'And all the time he's been lustin' after yeself, Anne—my God, did ye ever hear the like?'

Anne covered her face with her hands while Steynes managed to straighten himself up, gasping and dripping blood down the front of his jacket.

'What do you know about my wife, McGuire?' he muttered between breaths. 'You haven't had to live with her.'

'But she's had to live wid yeself, and suffer yer neglect!' shouted McGuire. 'That's a good woman ye've got there, a damned sight better than ye deserve—only ye've robbed her of all pride and self-esteem by yer treatment of her—enough to drive *anybody* to drink. Poor Monica!'

'How do you——? Where did you——?' stammered Steynes, blinking in astonishment while Anne listened in growing horror.

'I met Monica in Bristol when I'd taken a patient o' mine to see the same therapist,' McGuire snapped in explanation. 'She was just leavin', and looked so sad. We got talkin', and I took her to have some tea. It was then that I realised who she was. I promised on me honour that I'd never tell about her, and here I am now betrayin' her—though God knows I've wanted to tell *you*, Anne.'

Anne drew in a long breath as she learned the identity of the lady in the tea-shop. *Monica Steynes*. She recalled the sad, dark eyes of the woman now revealed as Steynes' wife—a suffering human being whom her husband had always dismissed as a burden that he had to bear. Anne's heart ached anew for her.

'Oh, Conor, I didn't know,' she whispered.

'Well, ye know now,' he rejoined briefly. Glancing at his watch, he turned to Steynes.

'The antenatal clinic'll be due to start soon. Will ye be fit to take it, Steynes, or shall I phone through to Bristol for a registrar?'

Even at a moment like this Anne noted Conor's concern for the mothers coming for their check-ups.

'I'll take my own clinic,' muttered Steynes.

McGuire nodded. 'Right, then I suggest ye go and tidy yeself up.'

He stood there, a tall figure beside the door, waiting for the surgeon to leave the office. Steynes looked at Anne, but she threw him a glare of such cold finality that he had no choice but to walk out with as much dignity as he could muster, dabbing a trickle of blood from his lower lip.

Anne turned imploringly to McGuire, but could not withstand the two blue searchlights that stared back at her as if at a stranger.

'Ye'd better go and compose yeself,' he advised tersely. 'It's a busy afternoon ye've got ahead o' ye.' And without further ado he left the office.

'Conor, please—wait a minute!' she called after his retreating back, but he strode down the corridor without turning his head.

Anne never knew how she got through the three-hour clinic session that afternoon, and had to summon up all her innate professionalism in order to hide her personal distress from the patients. She smiled as she checked blood-pressures, listened to foetal hearts, and placed her cool hands on the tummies of the women who lay on the examination couch. While she assessed the size and position of the babies she answered the mothers' questions, listened to their hopes and fears about labour and delivery, and reassured them with her usual wise advice.

Nevertheless she saw Wendy Garrett giving her some concerned looks, and overheard one or two of the more observant mothers remarking that the nice Miss Brittain looked rather strained. Anne fervently hoped that Wendy would not guess at a connection with Charles Steynes' silently subdued manner, most unlike his usual ebullience.

'He must have a boil on his face or something,' Anne heard one young mother-to-be saying. 'Why else would he have that plaster stuck on?'

'Could have cut himself shaving,' suggested her companion.

'Get away! A surgeon's supposed to have a steady hand. I wouldn't fancy being operated on by a man who can't even handle a razor!' said the first girl, to the accompaniment of suppressed giggles.

Anne kept her expression blank, and avoided exchanging any words with Steynes that were not absolutely necessary. Sister Garrett assisted him for most of the time but Anne had to act as chaperon when he saw Marjorie Stepford; he spent some time ascertaining the size of her baby at nearly thirty-four weeks of pregnancy. She had not gained weight during the past month, and he questioned her about her appetite and the amount of rest she took.

'We'd better ask for a repeat scan, and do some placental function tests,' he said with a frown. 'Will you make a note of that, Sister Brittain? Can Clive take you into Bristol tomorrow for the scan, Marjorie? Preferably in the morning, so that you don't miss your afternoon rest.'

'Why is he asking for these placental tests, Miss Brittain?' Marjorie asked, after blood samples had been taken in the Health Centre. 'There's nothing *wrong* with the placenta, is there?'

'I think he just wants to make absolutely sure that your baby's getting all the nourishment it needs,' Anne tried to explain, though she knew that Steynes suspected a degree of placental insufficiency, possibly due to hormonal imbalance.

'I haven't actually been feeling quite so good for the past couple of weeks,' admitted the doctor's wife. 'I've put it down to the heat. You don't feel like eating much in hot weather, do you?'

Anne tried to be cheerful and positive, pointing out that there were only another six weeks to go until the baby was due to be born. She knew that if the test results were not good Mr Steynes would order Marjorie into hospital, and might decide to induce labour a week or so earlier if the baby's environment was deteriorating. It was sometimes very difficult to explain matters truthfully to maternity patients without alarming them. She heaved an involuntary sigh, and Marjorie gave her a grateful look.

'You're such a comforting person to have around at a time like this, Miss Brittain. Give me a midwife rather than a doctor any day,' she said sincerely. 'I only wish that *you* were going to deliver my baby!'

Anne smiled and thanked her for the compliment, though she was in fact quite thankful that Marjorie was booked for the consultant delivery unit at Bristol, where she would be far safer if there were complications.

All the same, it was some comfort to know that her patients liked and trusted her, even though she had lost the respect of McGuire. Heaven only knew what he suspected about her and Steynes and, although Anne knew herself to be innocent of any illicit relationship with the man, she now blamed herself bitterly for her naïveté and stubborn refusal to heed the warnings of both McGuire and Miss Knight. She had been persistently blind to the signs of Steynes' ulterior motives; how the theatre nurses must have laughed at her stupidity—not that she cared about what they thought. No! It was Conor McGuire's look of icy contempt that she could not get out of her mind.

She did not see him again that day, nor on the Friday, when he had a half-day followed by a full weekend off duty. She overheard Dr Stepford saying that he had gone to visit his married sisters in the north, and would not return until late on Sunday night.

Anne felt that her brief dream of loving Conor McGuire was now well and truly shattered, and she steeled herself to forget the wonderful moments of closeness that they had shared at different times over the past two months—was it only that long? Tears filled her eyes when she was alone in her room and remembering the deep disappointment in his words and looks during that hateful scene with Steynes. She pictured a bleak future in which she would remain in her post until she became one of those grey-haired legendary figures that seemed to go on forever, while Conor would marry some suitable wife and she would see him become a family man. . .

Well, she would just have to be brave, that was all, and put her foolish dreams behind her, as Elaine Lester was doing. All right, so it wasn't easy, but it had to be done. The only thing she now really dreaded was the next Tuesday gynae operation list, when McGuire, Steynes and herself must work closely together as a team, behaving as if the shaming episode between them had never happened. Poor Anne went hot and cold at the very thought of it.

The weekend passed without incident, although whispers of some mysterious scandal passed between some members of the staff, and Anne had to face some questioning looks. She carried on with her work as normal, maintaining a dignified silence, though her heart sank as she went to her bed on the Monday night, knowing of the ordeal she must face in the operating-theatre the next day. She slept badly, and at about four o'clock leapt up in bed with a little cry of fear. Her bedside telephone was ringing.

'Miss Brittain? It's Sister Page here,' said the worried voice of the midwife on night duty. 'I've had a call from Mrs Stepford, who thinks she may be in premature labour.'

'What? Oh, yes—er—can't Clive take her to hospital in Bristol?' asked Anne, trying to collect her thoughts.

'That's the trouble—he isn't there. He's on call, and had to go out to a threatened miscarriage at Stone. Mrs Stepford thinks that her waters may have broken, and says she's getting pains. Of course she may be just panicking because she's on her own and it's her first baby—but do you think that somebody should go to see her?'

Anne thought quickly. If Marjorie was in labour at thirty-four weeks, things could happen very rapidly.

'Tell her to stay in bed, and I'll be with her just as soon as I can,' she rapped out. 'Get me a delivery pack and the portable incubator with the oxygen cylinder, and pray that I shan't need them!'

Within seven minutes flat Anne was dressed and hurrying down the stairs; in another three she had brought her car out of the garage and round to the front entrance. Sister Page dashed out with the equipment, which was stored away in the boot and, just as Anne was about to drive off, the sound of footsteps was heard hurrying from the Health Centre.

'What's up?' called McGuire, doing up his jacket buttons, and when the midwife hastily explained he dashed out of the front door, signaling Anne to wait for him.

'Two pairs o' hands'll be better than one if she's deliverin'—and if it's a false alarm, so much the better,' he gasped, settling into the passenger seat. Anne's concern for Marjorie overcame the embarrassment she felt at finding herself alone with this man.

'Clive will probably be back by the time we get there,' she said. 'Not that he won't be pleased to see us if she's really in premature labour.'

'There's some question o' placental insufficiency, isn't there? It'll be a tiddler, that's for sure,' he replied with a grimace, and Anne was thankful for his presence.

The eastern sky above Sunday's Hill shone with pure, clear light above the valley still buried in the grey shadows of night. Anne caught her breath

anew at the beauty of the summer dawn over
Gloucestershire, and stole a glance at her passenger
to see if he shared her thoughts. His profile was pale
against the light.

'It's a funny thing, but I was thinkin' about Marjorie
when I fell asleep,' he reflected, not taking his eyes
from the road. 'And then I suddenly woke up and I
swear I heard your footsteps on the stairs—though my
room is quite a way off—then I heard your car, so I
just threw some clothes on and rushed off as if the
hobs o' hell were after me. Marjorie needs us, that's
for sure,' he finished with a frown.

'Well, we're nearly there now,' replied Anne, aware
that all other considerations were set aside in their
shared mission to save life.

They were let in at the front door by a woman
neighbour who had been telephoned by Marjorie.

'Thank God!' she cried. 'She's *having* it; there's not
a minute to spare!'

They rushed after her as she led them upstairs to
the bedroom where Marjorie was sobbing and calling
for her husband. They pulled off their jackets and
hurried to her side.

'All right, Marjorie, we're here to take care of you
now,' smiled Anne, pulling back the duvet while Conor
began to open the delivery pack.

They were only just in time. Within two minutes a
tiny head appeared, the face an ominous bluish colour.
Anne immediately put her right forefinger beside its
neck, and gasped when she felt the loop of umbilical
cord tightly wound round it.

'Don't push for a minute, Marjorie—just take deep
breaths in and out,' she ordered, signalling to Conor
with a scissor movement of the fingers of her left hand.

'Quickly!' she urged in a whisper, then raising her voice she said to Marjorie, 'Don't push, just pant in and out—good girl.'

'Where in God's name are they?' muttered Conor, tearing the paper packaging in all directions to find the vital cord-scissors among the sterile towels, cotton-wool swabs and gauze squares. 'Oh, here they are!'

Anne snatched them from him and, placing a finger under the tight, shiny cord that encircled the child's neck in a stranglehold, she cut it through with a steady hand. The resulting spurt of blood was immediately controlled by Conor's application of two plastic cord-clamps, snapped on like clothes-pegs to each severed end. With one more expulsive contraction the body was born.

'Oh, Marjorie, you've got a little girl!' breathed Anne, always awed by the miracle of birth, no matter how many times she was privileged to witness it.

'Early one mornin', just as the sun was risin',' sang Conor, his eyes softening as he watched Anne pick up the baby and wrap her in a warm towel; the face was still slightly blue, and the tiny limbs moved jerkily.

'Thank you, Miss Brittain, you've delivered my baby after all!' said Marjorie shakily. 'We said we'd call her Jessica if she was a girl. Oh, do let me see her!'

Anne glanced at Conor who nodded assent, and the tiny but perfect form was gently placed in her mother's outstretched arms. Conor leaned over and flicked his forefingers against the soles of the little blue feet, while Anne blew short puffs of air on her face and chest.

It worked. The baby gasped, flexed her elbows and knees, and let out a howl of protest, unexpectedly loud for such a small infant. At hearing this welcome sound everybody relaxed, and the room was filled with rejoicing: Marjorie laughed, her neighbour wept, Anne almost groaned with relief, and Conor whistled an Irish jig.

'Whatever will her daddy say when he gets home?' wondered the neighbour, wiping her eyes.

'He'll hardly be congratulatin' us on our delivery technique, that's for sure,' observed Conor. 'We haven't so much as washed our hands. '*You* don't care, though, do you, Jessica? That's right, darlin', you have a good holler, I would if I were you!'

'How much does she weigh?' asked Marjorie. 'Is she *very* small?'

'About four pounds, at a guess, I'd say,' said Anne.

'We could weigh her on Marjorie's kitchen scales,' suggested Conor.

'Let's get the placenta out first,' insisted Anne firmly. 'And then we'll phone for an ambulance to take you both into hospital. Jessica will need to be seen by a paediatrician, and maybe she'll have——'

'Oh, please wait until Clive comes home!' begged Marjorie.

The neighbour hurried off to brew tea, then, five minutes after the baby's birth, the placenta was easily expelled, and Anne took it to the bathroom in a plastic bowl for inspection later. Within another five minutes an unsuspecting Clive Stepford arrived home and, seeing Anne's car outside and the lights on, he dashed up the stairs to behold a scene of general euphoria; he had eyes only for his wife, who was sitting up in bed holding their precious little daughter in her arms, and he rushed to her side and held mother and child in a silent embrace. Conor nodded to the neighbour that they should be left alone for a while and seizing Anne's hand he led her out of the room, closing the door behind them. They crossed the landing to the bathroom, luxuriously tiled in pink and beige.

'Anne, *mavourneen*, you were wonderful!' he told her. 'Listen, I've got to speak to you, and we've only got a couple o' minutes——'

Anne was unexpectedly overcome by shyness after the emotional intensity of the past hour.

'This was the culprit, you see,' she said, pointing to the undersized placenta with its stringy cord attached. 'Look at those infarcts where——'

'Oh, for God's sake, Anne, I can't be talkin' about placental infarcts now,' muttered Conor. 'Anne, Anne—I've been so angry, y'see. I was a man burned up with jealousy—sure, and I had murder in me heart for that man,' he confessed, the words tumbling out on top of each other. 'And the shame of it was that it wasn't really because of poor Monica, y'see—it was because o'—because o' *you*, Anne.'

He paused, and Anne could hardly take in what he had just said. She stood against the washbasin, waiting for him to explain further.

'It was the thought o' you bein' involved—bein' deceived, I should say, by the likes o' him, so unworthy o' you—I couldn't bear it, Anne, sure and I could not!'

There was no mistaking his meaning now, and Anne felt that she must seize this brief opportunity to clear up all misunderstandings.

'I never once gave Mr Steynes any encouragement, Conor, and I never suspected him, not even after what you said, I swear it,' she told him in agitation, her voice shaking. 'I've been a stupid, gullible fool, and I don't blame you for despising me for that, but I never for one moment thought that he was really intending to—— Oh, and that poor wife! How could I have been so stubborn, so——?' She turned away from him in a flood of helpless tears.

'Oh, please don't cry, my heart,' he begged, holding her close and drawing her head towards him so that her face was hidden against his shoulder. He rocked her in his arms as he bitterly reproached himself.

'Forgive me for bein' an arrogant fool, Anne—for settin' myself up as a judge o' you—you, of all people, the very best o' women. You must put it down to jealousy, Anne, the ragin' of a man who sees the woman he loves bein' claimed by somebody else with no right to her. Oh, darlin' Anne, I nearly went crazy, so I did!'

Standing there amid the incongruous surroundings of the bath, shower-cabinet, washbasin and toilet pedestal, a towel-rail along the wall and a chair on which stood the plastic bowl with the placenta in it, Anne experienced the delirious sensation of Conor's arms around her in a sheltering circle, and heard him saying unmistakable words of love—to her and no other woman. Raising her head, she lifted her tear-stained face to his, and in a moment his lips were upon hers in a drowning sweetness that was like nothing she had ever known. She clung to him, giving herself up to the exquisite closeness of his body, the warmth, the delicious maleness of him. Her limbs trembled and grew weak in his enfolding strength, and her world stood still when she heard him murmur, 'Heart of my heart. . .'

They scarcely heard the door open when Clive Stepford burst in on them, all smiles.

'Conor! Anne! How can I ever thank you two enough for——? Oh! Er, I'm so sorry——'

They drew apart, and his look of surprise was speedily replaced by a broad grin. Well! Whoever would have thought it? *Miss Brittain*!

CHAPTER NINE

THAT Tuesday passed like a dream for Anne, and her
feet seemed scarcely to touch the ground as she sailed
through the routine work, including Mr Steynes' operation list, which she no longer needed to dread. She
and Conor hid their elation beneath a formal theatre
protocol, and were careful to call each other Miss
Brittain and Dr McGuire, though an occasional secret
glance between them betrayed their special understanding. Charles Steynes silently progressed through
the list, and at coffee-time departed to his separate
room as usual. Anne could not help feeling a certain
sympathy for the man, who had after all suffered a
terrible blow to his self-esteem, and she could only
hope that some good might come out of it in time—
perhaps a new realisation of his wife's need for his
love, a willingness to listen to her pleas for understanding, rather than merely dismissing her as a problem.
Anne longed for Monica's sake that the marriage might
be revitalised and a fresh understanding reached; in
her own rejoicing heart she felt that there was no room
for grievances of any kind.

Or so she thought. . .

That evening Conor was officially on call, and with
Graham Sellars on holiday and Clive Stepford totally
preoccupied with his wife and new daughter in hospital
at Bristol, the Irish GP had no time to spend with
Anne. He was called out to a child having fits at a
house on a new estate, and to another child whose

parents thought he had eaten poisonous berries. When he had sorted out these problems Dr Sulliman was on the telephone, asking if there was a bed for a terminal admission he wanted to send in from Gloucester.

'Tomorrow evenin', Anne, *mavourneen*, we'll go for a walk over Sunday's Hill, but tonight you need a good rest,' he whispered as they stood in the entrance hall. She felt a kiss fall lightly on her forehead before he hurried away. She climbed the stairs to her flat, and after relaxing in a warm bath she thankfully got into bed, and was soon fast asleep under the duvet. It had been a very long day.

She was roused by a knock on her door; for a wild moment she thought it might be Conor, but it was Sister Winnie Mason who stood before her, still in uniform and with a strange expression on her motherly features.

'Sister Mason! You should have been home hours ago!' exclaimed Anne in surprise.

'I know, Miss Brittain, but I've had a busy evening over there,' replied Winnie, searching Anne's face as if trying to make up her mind how best to break some news. 'We've had an admission, Miss Brittain,' she said gravely, 'sent in by Dr Sulliman, and in a very bad way.'

'Oh, yes, Dr McGuire was saying something about a terminal patient coming into the annexe,' nodded Anne, instantly alerted. 'Do they need a special nurse?'

'Miss Brittain—Anne—there's something I've got to tell you, my dear,' said the sister, with unusual familiarity for her. Her eyes were full of sympathy, and Anne suddenly felt a shiver of alarm.

'What is it, Winnie? Tell me at once! Oh, my God, is it my mother? Tell me!' Her voice rose in fear.

'All right, Anne, it's not your mother,' replied Winnie Mason. 'It's your father.'

Anne stood as still as a statue; her face was drained of colour.

'Don't try to break it gently, just tell me,' she ordered. 'We're talking about this new admission, right?'

'Yes, Anne. He's known as James Calvert. Jimmy.'

Anne stiffened at hearing this name. 'Go on.'

'He was picked up in Gloucester by a voluntary organisation for the homeless,' said Winnie Mason in some embarrassment. 'He's been—er—sleeping rough, it seems, and has acute brocho-pneumonia and advanced emphysema. His lungs are in a shocking state——'

She broke off at the sight of Anne's stricken face.

'Oh, no. *No*,' whispered Anne, then nodded to the sister to go on.

'They took him to a hostel to start with, then found that there was no vacancy in the acute medical ward of the nearest hospital, so Dr Sulliman asked if we could take him. Dr McGuire agreed, especially when Dr Sulliman told him that Jimmy was a Stretbury man.'

'A very long time ago,' muttered Anne. 'Er—does Dr McGuire have any idea who——?'

'No. I didn't say a word.'

Anne looked hard at the sister. 'But *you* knew who he was, Winnie?'

'Yes, as soon as I saw him I knew straight away. He's pitifully changed, but I knew Stanley Brittain. Your mother and I were both courting at the same time, and used to meet our——' She broke off and sighed. 'And *you'll* know your dad, my dear, when you see him.'

'I don't want to see him.' Anne's mouth was set in a hard, straight line. 'If he wasn't terminally ill I'd telephone Dr Sulliman and ask for him to be transferred somewhere else. Anywhere else but here.'

'Anne!' The sister was shocked by this unfamiliar Miss Brittain who stood before her, pale and glacial.

'I'm not going to be sentimental or hypocritical about this, Sister Mason,' went on Anne in a voice of ice. 'That man made my poor mother's life a misery. He didn't want to be lumbered with a family, and I'm not prepared to call him Father now.' She took a step towards the open-mouthed Winnie Mason, and spoke with deliberation. 'And another thing—my mother is not to be bothered over this. She's been through enough unhappiness because of him and is not to be told that he's turned up here. The fewer people who know, the better.'

'But she will have to be told!' cried Winnie. 'She has a right to know. He—he won't live long, and if I know Lilian Brittain she'll want to come and——'

'She is *not* to be told!' ordered Anne as they stood and faced each other. 'I forbid you to tell her. Look, Winnie, I know that you will care for—James Calvert, and see that he gets everything he's entitled to as a patient in his condition. I don't want to see him myself, and I shall not come over to the annexe while he's—while he's still in there. I can't face that man. I'm sorry, but I *can't*!'

All at once her self-control faltered, and she sat down on her bed, trembling from head to foot. Winnie sat down beside her and put a tentative arm around her tense shoulders.

'My dear Anne——'

'*No*! I know how shocking this must seem to you,

Winnie, but you never had to live with Stanley Brittain. And don't use that name, please. He called himself Calvert, and he can be known as Calvert. It was his so-called stage name.'

'All right then, Anne, but I'm a nurse first and foremost, not a judge,' answered Winnie quietly. 'I'm sorry to have brought you such unwelcome news. I can promise you that my staff will do everything possible to make his last hours as comfortable as we can.'

'I know you will. Thank you.' Anne averted her head, and Sister Mason saw that she was undergoing a tumultuous inward struggle. After a moment or two of silence the middle-aged Sister rose, and buttoned the light navy jacket she wore over her uniform. 'I must go home now, it's getting very late. You know, Anne, you're going to have to come to terms with this relationship. You've been given a wonderful opportunity to make your peace with your father, but there's not much time left for you to take it.'

'Good night, Sister Mason,' said Anne without looking up.

When Winnie had left the flat, Anne covered her face with her hands and gave way to a dry, painful sob of unresolved bitterness. Oh, why had he been sent here of all places? Of all the cruel strokes of fate!

Conor had managed to get a few hours' sleep, but a call to an asthmatic woman just before six took him several miles up the A38 to Berkeley. Having calmed the patient's panic and reassured her that she was not about to die, he chatted over a cup of tea with her and her husband before leaving. It was a glorious morning, and on his way back he could not resist parking in a lane and taking a quick climb up Sunday's

Hill, drinking in deep breaths of the delicious fresh air
and feasting his eyes on the green patchwork of field
and meadow below the steep rise on which he strode,
a solitary but exultant figure. Conor was feeling extra-
ordinarily pleased with life; he was in that delightful
state of preoccupation with another person which is
usually referred to as being in love.

He remembered Anne's tears, her smiles, the sweetness of her lips as she had clung to him in that brief
moment after the birth of the Stepfords' baby. . .there
were no doubts in his mind. As his fortieth birthday
approached with a sense of time marching on he knew
what he wanted more than anything else in the world.
Looking across to Stretbury Memorial's grey roof, just
visible above the trees, he whispered her name to the
passing breeze: Miss Bossy-boots! The indispensable
Miss Anne Brittain! Conor laughed out loud at himself—it was good to be alive.

Before going in to breakfast on his arrival back at
the hospital, he headed for the Hylton Annexe to check
on the new admission of the previous evening. The
man's haunted brown eyes had struck a chord somewhere in his heart, and he longed to be able to bring
some comfort to the last stages of Jimmy Calvert's
journey. Might there not be a relative who could
be sent for, or a not-forgotten friend from the past?
Conor was strangely troubled by the homeless,
friendless man.

The night nurse on duty reported that Jimmy had
slept for short periods on continuous oxygen inhalation
and had taken a little warm milk from a feeding-cup
that morning. Conor stood looking down at the
emaciated frame, the skin roughened and deeply
begrimed by the effects of sleeping rough throughout

the winter months. At least he now lay between clean sheets on a comfortable bed, thought the doctor; nourishment and antibiotics might delay the end for a short time, though irreparable damage had been done.

'How're you feelin' now, Jimmy old friend? Any better this mornin'?' asked Conor softly.

The patient opened one eye. He tried to clear his throat, but his voice was hoarse, a barely intelligible whisper.

'Lily,' he muttered. 'Lily—where is she?' Two filmy eyes fixed on Conor, who felt that he had seen this face before somewhere. Or did Jimmy remind him of someone he already knew?

'Who's Lily, Jim? Where does she live?' he asked, glancing at the night nurse, who shrugged. A glimmer of hope appeared on the ravaged features, but then Jimmy's eyes closed, as if he was exhausted by the effort of speaking in addition to the labour of breathing.

McGuire beckoned the nurse out into the corridor where the residents were making their way to the dining-room for breakfast.

'I'll have a word with Miss Brittain and see if she knows of any Calverts in Stretbury,' he said. 'And Sister Mason's another one who might remember somebody of that name. Sure, and between them they must come up with somethin'!'

But Anne was closeted in her office with her secretary, and she was on the telephone when he tried to see her before his morning surgery. She did not appear in the dining-room at lunchtime, and Sister Barr told him that Miss Brittain had asked her to take charge of the hospital for the afternoon; Anne had gone to her room to rest, and was not to be disturbed except for a grave emergency. Conor was puzzled, and actually telephoned Anne's room; there was no answer. In actual fact, she lay on her bed with the curtains drawn, staring at the ceiling and trying unsuccessfully to come to terms with the resentment and chagrin that her father's reappearance had caused her.

Returning to her office at five, she found McGuire waiting for her. All the pleasure she would normally have felt on seeing him was lost in the grey fog of her emotional crisis, and she did not smile. Her secretary had told him that Miss Brittain did not seem her usual self today, and had whispered in his ear that she thought Miss Brittain was upset about the new admission to the annexe.

'Oh, no, not again!' he had exclaimed, though his blue eyes betrayed his amusement. 'Gettin' patients into that place is like smugglin' refugees ashore under cover o' darkness!'

He greeted Anne with a broad smile, already prepared for some opposition.

And he got it.

'I feel that Dr Sulliman should have tried harder to get that patient into somewhere nearer Gloucester,' she said flatly. 'And you should not have been so ready to accept him into our emergency bed. I'd arranged for an elderly lady to come into the annexe this week for a short stay, to give her daughter a break. Now, with the last bed gone, I shall have to go back on my word.'

Conor was chilled by the unfriendliness of her tone, and taken aback by her white face and dark-ringed eyes.

'Is this really yourself I'm hearin', Anne?' he asked

softly. 'Would you have me turn away a poor old guy down on his luck, dyin' o' the pewmoney and heaven knows what besides?'

'Yes, what else besides?' retorted Anne. 'What kind of infection might he have brought in to my elderly residents? He could be HIV positive, for all you know, or be full of TB with his lifestyle. I'm very annoyed about the whole business.'

There was silence for a moment while Conor considered how best he should react to this angry woman. He had admitted to himself that he loved her, and this uncharacteristic behaviour did not make him love her any the less. On the contrary, he felt it was his responsibility to find out the reason for it in a sensitive way. He smiled, giving the secretary a polite nod of dismissal and closing the door behind her.

Anne stood, clenching her hands at her sides, forbidding herself to give way to what she saw as weakness, and not meeting his eyes for fear of bursting into tears. He resisted a strong urge to put his arms around her and force her to face him; some sixth sense warned him to tread carefully, and a memory came back to him of their earlier conversation about Henry Dodswell and his daughter. He had been aware then of a deep hurt somewhere in Anne's past, and had not felt justified in pressing her then; now he again sensed a need for caution.

'Come, now, what's the matter, darlin'?' he asked softly, and when she did not answer he went on in a conversational way, 'I just don't believe you'd send a dyin' man from your door, Anne, no matter what you say. And seemin'ly he did live in Stretbury once. D'you know of any Calverts livin' around here?'

'There are none that I know of,' she said quickly.

'Hmm. Does the name Lily ring a bell with you?'

'Not at all. And now, if you'll excuse me, Conor, I've got work to do, and a splitting headache, which doesn't help. I shan't be staying up late tonight.'

'I'm sorry to hear that, Anne. It's been a gruellin' time for you, one way and another. I've got a lot of jobs to catch up with, too.' He spoke with deliberate good humour that belied his inward concern for her. 'I'll see you around, then, Anne—OK?'

She did not answer.

In the office of the Hylton Annexe that evening, McGuire confronted a worried and defensive Sister Mason.

'It's about Jimmy Calvert,' she told him, clasping and unclasping her hands. 'It's no good, Dr McGuire, I just have to obey my conscience.'

'Of course you must, Winnie,' he smiled. 'What about him?'

'You won't say I told you anything, will you, Doctor?' she begged.

'That I never would, Winnie. You do know him, then?'

'Yes, I do. And I've just got to let his—his relatives know,' she confessed, to Conor's great relief.

'Ah! Good girl that ye are. Now, how can I help? Have you got an address or a phone number?'

'I could get hold of—of the right person,' said Winnie evasively, and McGuire was aware of a mystery somewhere, of information being withheld.

'It's important that we don't delay, Winnie,' he told her seriously. 'There isn't much that can be done now for Jimmy's physical condition, so his emotional needs are paramount. If ever I saw a soul in torment lookin'' out of a man's eyes——' He shook his head and sighed deeply.

She called to an experienced nursing auxiliary on duty that evening, and quietly asked her to take charge of the annexe for half an hour.

'No need to tell Miss Brittain,' McGuire heard her say as she put on her navy jacket and hurried out. It was strictly forbidden for sisters in charge of a ward to leave the building while on duty, and McGuire's sense of disquiet deepened; there were troubling mysteries here, and he felt that he was being excluded from some dark secret. He went to take his evening surgery in the Health Centre, but hurried back as soon as he possibly could, asking Elaine Lester to take over the remainder of his patients when he saw that she had finished her own surgery.

'You're an angel, Elaine,' he muttered gratefully. 'Not many left to see, and no major problems—but I have to get back to the annexe, y'see.'

'It's quite all right, Dr McGuire, I'm perfectly happy to help out if you're needed elsewhere,' Elaine assured him with a professional air, very different from the eager enthusiasm she would have shown a couple of weeks earlier.

Conor flew along the corridor, across the central area and down the covered passage to the annexe. He was met by a tearful Winnie Mason at the door of Calvert's room, while in the corridor sat Matthew Crawford, looking far from pleased.

'I don't think they should have sent for her, Dr McGuire,' he grumbled when he saw his GP. 'It's not as if he was ever any good to her, is it?'

McGuire had no idea what the cross old man was talking about, and raised his eyebrows towards Winnie

Mason in a silent question. She put a finger to her lips and pointed to the door, which was ajar. McGuire put his head round it, and saw and understood everything in an instant.

Mrs Lilian Brittain was sitting beside the bed, holding her husband's bony hand in hers. She was smiling and speaking softly, assuring him that she had forgiven him long ago and that he was not to worry. Tears ran down her cheeks at the sight of the face that now gazed up at her so gratefully, as if he could never see enough of the wife he had deserted. His breathing was painful and rasping, but he repeated her name between gasps.

'Lily—my lovely Lily—never lucky after—after I left my Lily——'

'Don't try to talk, Stan,' Conor heard Lilian say. 'That's all over and done with now, you poor old boy.'

McGuire turned away, moved by the sheer goodness of the woman, and full of pity for the wreck of humanity now revealed as Anne's father. *Of course*, he thought, how could I not have guessed? If I hadn't been so sure that her father was dead, I'd have known straight away—she's got his eyes. McGuire recalled that Anne had not actually told him a lie, he had just received a false impression that she had not corrected. He felt that he now understood her present emotional conflict—the hurt of her father's desertion, the shame of his abandonment of family responsibilities. In thinking of her father as dead, she could not cope with his return from that convenient oblivion. Conor's heart ached for her.

'I think Anne Brittain should be here,' he said quietly to Sister Mason. 'I'll go and fetch her.'

'Don't bank on her coming, Doctor,' warned the sister. 'And don't tell her it was my doing, will you?'

'Don't worry, she can blame me—I can take it!' He grinned as he hurried off to the main building in search of the Senior Nursing Administrator.

He found her in the women's ward, sitting beside a patient who had been on yesterday's operation list. When he beckoned to her she rose and came towards him slowly, her pale features reflecting the turmoil within.

'Can we talk, Miss Brittain? I think your office would be best, out of earshot o' these ladies.' He lowered his voice and spoke close to her ear. 'Come along now, there's a darlin'. Sure and there's nothin' to worry about, you'll see.'

She gave a slight nod, and followed him out of the ward and into the corridor, where they crossed the parquet floor to her office. She unlocked the door and they went in; he closed the door behind them and she sat down at her desk, indicating the chair on the other side, but he picked up a small chair and brought it to sit beside her.

'Go ahead, Conor. I suppose it's to do with the patient in the annexe,' she said in a low voice. 'Of course I shouldn't have said what I did. I apologise. Put it down to pressure of work and—the trouble last week.'

'That's my good girl. And I want to tell you that I don't blame you, Anne, for feelin' the way you do about your dad.'

Anne was almost relieved to hear these words. Of course he had to know, and so must the whole hospital, inevitably; so must the whole of Stretbury in a short while, she thought wretchedly.

She turned to face him, her eyes two dark, mournful pools. Again McGuire had to fight the urge to enfold her in his arms, and simply took hold of her hands which felt cold in spite of the warm evening.

'Who told you?' she asked. 'I suppose Sister Mason's been telling things she had no business to.'

'Winnie Mason told me nothin', Anne, and only did what she should. Listen, darlin', whatever the man's done, if your mother can forgive him, so can you. Come with me now, and——'

'*My mother?*' cried Anne, her eyes widening even further. 'Is *she* with him? Who told her? *Who?*' The threatening look on her face would have daunted a lesser man.

'Who told her is neither here nor there, Anne. The fact is that she wanted to be with him, settin' his mind at rest, makin' her peace with him, just as you're goin' to, *mavourneen*.'

She almost leapt from her chair and stood over him, her eyes blazing.

'No, Conor, no! I'm not going to say anything to that man, and you have no right to ask me—you just don't understand the circumstances!' she ground out through clenched teeth.

'Oho, and where have I heard *that* before?' he returned with a smile. 'Sure now, and I remember— it was over my Uncle Harry and his daughter. Now that was an interestin' case, wasn't it?'

'Damn you, McGuire, this is *nothing* like the Dodswells!' she almost shouted, and Conor braced himself. For a moment he thought she might strike him, but she turned away and continued speaking in an agitated tone.

'My mother was hurt and humiliated beyond belief by that man, what with his fancy women and his drinking, his debts and his overblown ideas about acting—

oh, don't talk to me about him, Conor, just don't
talk to me!'

Her voice rose hysterically, and Conor looked at her
with deep compassion, seeing the unhappiness beneath
the fury.

'Anne, please sit down again, there's a darlin', and
tell your Uncle Conor all about it,' he said very gently,
and to his relief she sank down on the chair beside him,
putting her hand to her face in a gesture of despair. He
felt sure that his battle was halfway won.

'That's better,' he said encouragingly. 'I'm here and
listenin', Anne. So, we've established that your dad
was a drinker and a womaniser and didn't support
his family—and, worst of all, he flopped on the
stage o' the Bristol Old Vic. Anythin' else to add
against him?'

She raised her head in a quick gesture.

'Don't try to make it sound funny, Conor, because
it wasn't. After putting my mother through hell he
walked out on us all, with some actress who left him
as soon as she saw that he was never going to be the
big star he thought he was. He took up with various
women who spent his money while our mother
struggled to bring up Edward and myself on what she
could earn. His luck must have finally run out, and so
did the women. I didn't know he'd reached street level,
sleeping rough with the down-and-outs—my God!'

She looked straight at McGuire, her mouth set, her
eyes darkly shadowed.

'No, Conor. Don't ask me to forget and forgive. If
my mother can, that's because of the way she's made.
I'm different, and I can't. You don't understand what
you're asking me to do—you've never had to forgive
something like this!'

'Oh, Anne, Anne! That's all *you* know—you don't know what you're sayin', girl!' There was reproach in the words, though he held out his arms to her; she evaded him, turning away and hiding her face.

'*No*, Conor! I don't want your pity, or any other man's—I don't trust men,' she said with fierce bitterness. 'I've got my work, and I don't need a man in my life, thank you very much.'

He drew in a sharp, painful breath as he realised at last the extent of the damage done to this woman by her father's rejection. He decided that shock tactics were now needed. Seizing her arm, he pulled her roughly towards him, forcing her to pay attention.

'I won't have ye sayin' that, woman! Are ye thinkin' ye're the only soul in the world wid a grievance? Look outside yeself, Anne!'

The deep voice broadened into the brogue of his childhood, and Anne shrank from the sight of his chalk-white face. His eyes were two burning blue points, almost frightening in their intensity.

'Conor, don't look like that—I never meant to say that, I——' she began.

'No, Miss Brittain, maybe ye didn't, but now ye can just listen to *me* for a change. I've been patient wid ye up to now over the sorry business o' yer father— and by the way, yer mother's a happier woman than yeself right now, for showin' mercy to a penitent man at the last—but I'm not goin' to be told that I don't understand about forgivin'! No way!'

Anne actually forgot her own inner turmoil as she stared at this new aspect of Conor McGuire, and she found that she very much wanted to know what could make him look and sound like this embattled man. She laid a hand upon his arm.

'All right, I'll listen, Conor! Tell me, and I'll listen,' she said, quietly.

He walked over to the open window, looking out at the hospital gardens in the calm light of evening. The song of birds drifted in, and the scent of the honeysuckle she had trained up the wall to her office window. Conor's rigid back was towards her, his shoulders tensely hunched; she sat and waited with bated breath in the silence.

At last he began to speak, slowly and from the depths of his heart, keeping his face to the window.

'There were six of us, three boys and three girls, growin' up on a small farm in Donegal,' he said quietly. 'Our parents weren't well off, and we didn't have many luxuries, but we were happy—a bit wild, maybe, but it was a good life in the country—a backwater compared to Stretbury. My brother Aidan was destined for the priesthood from the start, and I always wanted to be a doctor. We were lucky to win scholarships, and I did all sorts of odd jobs to get myself up to university and medical school. Even so, we couldn't have made it, Aidan and myself, without our parents helpin' us out, scrimpin' and scrapin' every bit o' money together for us.'

There was a pause while he seemed to struggle to find the right words.

'And there was our youngest brother, Bernard, in many ways the best o' the bunch. He was no academic, but a country boy through and through. He knew the note of every wild bird, and could call to them and they'd answer—they'd come and sit on his shoulder. He could milk a cow when he was ten years old, and he had a way with all animals—a fully grown bull or a farrowin' sow, they'd never go for Bernard. He'd

talk to them and he'd touch them, and they'd know
he was their friend. We used to call him St Francis,
just jokin', like. Oh, he was somebody special, Anne.
I'll never meet his like again.'

He was silent for a minute, and Anne went over to
stand beside him at the window, her heart sinking with
dismay; she knew that she was about to hear how he
had lost this brother.

'You don't have to tell me all this, Conor,' she whispered, dreading what she must hear.

'Ah, but I *do* have to tell you, Anne, because you
think I don't understand about havin' to forgive, y'see.
I don't talk about Bernard much now, only to Aidan
and our sisters, especially Ciara when I visit her at the
convent. And now I have to tell *you*, Anne.'

She made no reply, but gently placed a hand on
his shoulder. He did not turn round as he continued
his story.

'I got my medical degree before Aidan was ordained,
and I had this crazy idea that I should go to Belfast,
to work among the victims o' the violence there. I'd
done an anaesthetics house job in Dublin, and I got
very interested in the subject o' pain relief—whether
in illness or childbirth or injury. I loved it in Belfast,
Anne, I really did—went from senior houseman to a
registrarship in anaesthetics—the sleep o' life!'

Again he paused, and Anne let her head rest against
his shoulder while her heart yearned over him.

'Came my thirtieth birthday, and Aidan and Bernard
made their way up to Belfast to celebrate it with me.
Aidan was workin' in Derry then, doin' a grand job
buildin' bridges between the different denominations.
Ah, we had such hopes o' what we'd achieve in those
days, Anne! Bernard was twenty-one, a great big lad,

but gentle and trustin', like. He was about to enter the pub where we'd arranged to meet up when all of a sudden he heard a shot fired, and this masked gunman came hurtlin' out of the pub and ran straight into him. A motorcyclist was waitin' for this guy, so as to make a quick getaway, and Bernard realised there'd been a shootin' inside the pub. He held on to this gunman and said somethin' about no good comin' o' guns and bombs—the poor lad didn't know the sort o' people he was dealin' with, y'see.'

Conor stopped speaking, and Anne put her arms around him and held him tightly as he stood with his back to her, her hands clasped together over his white coat. The scene he described was more real to her than the room in which they stood, and she truly shared the agony of it.

'And was—was Bernard——?' she asked softly, unable to finish the question.

'Yes, Anne, he was shot—fatally. The guy in the pub who'd been shot, the real target, he recovered—but my brother died. People came pourin' out o' the pub, yellin' and cursin', but all I saw when I got there was my brother lyin' on the pavement in his own blood, and Aidan giving him the Last Sacrament. Oh, Anne, I'm tellin' ye, I know what it is to hate—and to swear that I'll never forgive!'

A huge sob shook his frame, and Anne's tears fell too as she held him. Still he did not turn round.

'It was a tragedy for our family in every way,' he continued brokenly. 'Bernard was to have taken over the farm, y'see. Dad never got over his death, and he started drinkin'. That's still a problem, and my mother sometimes has a hard time of it with him, though you never hear her complainin'.'

'So—that was why you left Belfast and went to sea?' prompted Anne sadly.

'That's right. I couldn't stay there after that. Life in the Merchant Navy was rough at times, and I did a fair bit o' drinkin' myself, too, for a time. It was Aidan who helped me to come to terms with losin' Bernard, to accept that these things happen when there's sectarian hatred; innocent people get killed and nobody cares—or so it seemed to us McGuires. The headlines said, "21-year-old Man Killed in Latest Sectarian Shoot-Out"—as if he'd been one o' them, fightin' and brawlin', which he never did.'

'Oh, Conor, don't say any more!' wept Anne against his back, her face buried in his white coat.

'No, Anne, you must listen to me, because I'm comin' to the most important bit,' he answered, taking a couple of deep breaths to compose himself before continuing.

'Bernard's death could have destroyed me, Anne, and it very nearly did finish me as a doctor. Aidan worked hard on me, and brought me to the point where I knew I had to forgive the gunman who shot Bernard, even to see him as a man more in need o' mercy and salvation than my brother who was only after tryin' to make peace, God rest his soul. Believe me, Anne, it wasn't easy, in fact it was a terrible struggle, but I came to my knees at last and asked for the poison to be taken away from my heart. And it was, thanks be to God—I found I could carry on again, and after five years in the Merchant Navy I worked as surgical registrar and anaesthetist in different city hospitals. Aidan's a parish priest in Belfast, but I couldn't go back there. Then I thought I'd try my hand at general practice in a rural area—and here I am!'

With these words Conor turned round at last and faced her; with one movement they were in each other's arms, their eyes closed, the tears still wet on their cheeks. It was a moment of healing for Anne, and she felt a great sense of release, even after Conor's tragic story.

Shyly she felt for his hand and held it as she gently released herself from his arms.

'Thank you, Conor. It must have cost you a great deal to relive that terrible day, just for my sake,' she said with humility in her soft brown eyes.

'I'll be rewarded, *mavourneen*, when I see you at your father's bedside,' he answered.

'Will you come with me, Conor?'

His only answer was to kiss her forehead, and still holding hands they walked out of the office and towards the covered passageway leading to the Hylton Annexe. When they reached the door of Stanley Brittain's room Lilian was just leaving; she looked up with a smile at her daughter.

'Ah, there you are, dear. I knew you'd come,' she said, apparently without surprise. 'I've telephoned Edward, and he's driving down from Birmingham this evening.' Then she stood aside to let Anne take her place beside Stanley Brittain.

Anne could not suppress a gasp of shock at his appearance, and once again her tears overflowed.

'Hello, Dad. It's Anne. I—I've come to see you, Dad.'

A thin hand reached out to her, two sunken eyes looked up imploringly, afraid that she might vanish like a dream. Then she was leaning over him, touching his worn, grey features, kissing his heavily lined forehead.

'All right, Daddy, all right, don't cry,' she whispered. 'Everything's finished now, it's all right.'

Stanley was by this time too weak to speak, but his eyes saw the forgiveness freely granted without need of words; their mutual smiles and tears were more eloquent than any speeches, and peace filled Anne's heart in that solemn moment of reconciliation.

The precious minutes had to be curtailed when her father's breathing became difficult, and continuous oxygen had to be recommenced. Anne herself repositioned the plastic mask over his nose and mouth, and she helped Winnie to sit him up higher on his bank of pillows. Conor watched from the doorway, and decided to send for the priest from St Joseph's church to administer the Last Sacrament to a man now at peace after a troubled life.

When Anne rose from the bedside, she gave Conor a tearful smile.

'Oh, Conor,' she told him. 'When I think how much I was dreading it, as soon as I actually saw him lying there, it was so easy to forgive everything. Thank you. I feel as if I've been set free from the past!'

He smiled and held her lightly against him as her mother and Winnie Mason walked together down the corridor. Stanley Brittain was now sleeping, and McGuire looked long and thoughtfully at the man who had thrown away his life's happiness.

'Poor old bastard,' he muttered.

Anne gave him a questioning look.

'Nothin', just sayin' a little prayer for him, that's all,' he assured her.

Edward Brittain arrived a little later, but by then Stanley had slipped into unconsciousness, and Edward sat at the bedside holding his father's hand and giving him a kiss of farewell. Though naturally upset by the circumstances, Edward confided to Anne that he had really only come to please their mother. Being the younger of the two, he had less traumatic memories of their father's desertion, and had been protected by his mother and sister from the emotional shock of it. He left with his mother to stay the night at the bungalow, and Anne went to her bed, where she at once fell into an exhausted, dreamless sleep.

The call came from Night Sister Pilgrim just before dawn, and Conor got up to join the three who stood beside Stanley Brittain as his life ended peacefully, following the reconciliation with his family.

Anne was ordered to take two weeks' compassionate leave, and spent the time at her mother's home, preparing meals, receiving visitors, and generally helping her mother through the days before the funeral— delayed due to the need for an inquest. She was overwhelmed by the enormous number of cards and gifts of flowers, fruit and confectionery that arrived for them from the staff of the hospital, and she was deeply touched by the loving thoughts from many ex-patients and the residents of the Hylton Annexe, who sent a beautiful floral arrangement with a card signed by them all. It was brought to the bungalow by Miss Victoria Knight, driven there in Conor's Fiat.

On his part, Conor sensed that it would be inappropriate to make any declaration of his love for Anne at such a time. She was physically and emotionally exhausted, and he took care that his daily visits were those of a devoted friend rather than a lover. The other regular visitor was Matthew Crawford, who quietly busied himself in the garden while Lilian sat in a deckchair. It was a time of waiting and restoration.

When the quiet funeral took place at St Joseph's church, Matthew and Conor discreetly supported Lilian and Anne, who walked on each side of Edward. Apart from Winnie Mason and Lady Hylton there were no other mourners. Anne felt that a chapter in their lives had closed, and she now longed to return to take up her work once again.

It was on the last evening of Anne's leave that Conor came to suggest that he and Anne should take their long-deferred walk over Sunday's Hill; Anne's eager face and shining eyes assured him that his timing was perfect. She changed into a pretty cotton button-through dress, and picked up a light jacket to put on if the breeze grew cool.

Settling into the passenger seat of the Fiat, Anne was conscious of a new contentment in her heart, thanks to this man who had bared his very soul in order to make her change her attitude towards her father and be freed from the restraints of the past. She not only understood Conor better now, but also herself; she saw that she was no different after all from the great majority of women. Not only was she capable of forgiving, but she was now ready to give her love unreservedly to a man, and to receive his love in return with joy and thankfulness. And that man was here beside her, freed at last from all misunderstandings between them; on this heavenly summer evening Anne walked on a pinnacle of happiness.

He parked the car in a layby near to a farm gate, and they walked hand in hand up to the ridge where Conor had taken his early morning walk. A copse of tall old trees crowned the summit, and in the middle of this was a grassy clearing, as perfect a spot as any lovers could desire.

He put his arm around her waist as they climbed the last few yards and emerged from the trees into the open space under the purpling sky of twilight. The air was warm and fragrant, and Conor pointed to the evening star. The silence was broken by the early calls of night birds and the myriad soft rustlings and scamperings of little animals who felt safe to come out of hiding at this hour; a family of rabbits scattered at their approach, but presently returned to their nocturnal rituals.

Conor seized her arm and turned her round to face him.

'Anne, you know what I have to say to you,' he breathed urgently. 'So many things have delayed me, and now it's more than time——'

'Yes, Conor?' She smiled up at him. 'Tell me, I'm listening.'

'Anne, my heart is at your feet, for you to take up or cast away,' he whispered.

Anne replied, 'My heart has always missed a beat whenever I saw you, Conor, right from when we first met. Oh, Conor, how you have changed me!'

He bent his head to kiss her, and instantly a fire blazed within them both, sweeping away caution in its enveloping flames. Eventually Anne wrenched her lips from his, and looked up into his face, her eyes alight with the love she no longer felt the need to hide.

'I've waited so long for this, Conor, and I still can't believe it's true,' she told him, putting her arms up around his neck. 'Prove to me that it's real—make love to me, Conor. We'll go back to my flat—or yours——'

Conor was almost irresistibly persuaded; he closed his eyes as her body trembled in his arms.

'Now don't be temptin' me, my heart, for it's meself

who wants you more than words can tell,' he parried, each word dragged out of him with the effort of resistance.

Anne laughed softly, putting a finger over his mouth and whispering her pent-up passionate yearning close to his ear. Conor was surprised and deeply moved by her unreserved trust, and he was most sorely tempted to yield to their mutual need. . . But with a super-human effort he struggled to overcome the dictates of desire.

'Anne—oh, Anne, *mavourneen*, once we're married I'll ask for nothin' more out o' life,' he told her in a voice that was nearly a groan. 'But my darlin', you'll be glad you waited until—until you're really Mrs McGuire. It'd be a risk, for one thing, and sure, you might wish that we hadn't——'

'Conor, I'm not worried about it, can't you see?' she assured him, but he kissed her and said that it was for her sake that they must wait. Walking slowly down the hill with their arms around each other's waists, Anne knew that she had never loved him more than at this moment. She sensed that he truly understood her, and wanted nothing but what was best for her, and because of this his usually impulsive nature was restrained by a caution that was normally hers. Their love had apparently changed their roles, and by his carefulness towards her he had proved his love more truly than by seizing the opportunity of the moment, with possible regret later.

When they kissed goodnight in the deserted entrance hall at the foot of the stairs leading up to Anne's flat she clung to him fiercely. Her eyes glowed like jewels in the dim light, overflowing with the love she felt for him.

'Let's get married *soon*, Conor—we don't need to have a big wedding, do we?'

'Just as soon as Father Hopkinson can set it up for us, my heart—or in God's name I'll be forgettin' me saintly virtue, and that's a fact!'

The wedding of Miss Brittain to Dr McGuire took place at St Joseph's church in Stretbury on a golden afternoon in early August. The ceremony was conducted by the bridegroom's brother, Father Aidan McGuire, and Conor's parents came over from Donegal; his sisters, brothers-in-law, nephews and nieces occupied three pews, while on the bride's side sat Mrs Brittain with her daughter-in-law and two grandchildren. Matthew Crawford was seated discreetly behind the lady who would soon become his wife.

The doctors from the practice were there too, with their wives. Dr Lester was on call, but managed to slip into the church just in time for the marriage ceremony. She had been astounded by the news of McGuire's choice, and realised that she had underestimated Anne as a woman. Lady Hylton also had mixed feelings as she took her place near to the aisle for a good view.

Gasps of admiration greeted the bride as she appeared on her brother Edward's arm, a radiant figure in a white silk wedding-gown and gauzy veil, carrying a bouquet of yellow and white roses. The brilliance of her shining dark eyes and the sweetness of her softly curving mouth caused some of her colleagues to stare in surprise at 'Miss Bossy-boots', and admit that Conor McGuire knew a good-looking woman when he saw one.

Anne's heart swelled at the sight of so many friends and colleagues who had come to see her married, and she smiled joyously to left and right as Edward led her slowly up the aisle towards the tall figure who waited for her at the chancel steps with Clive Stepford, his best man. Anne saw Marjorie in the congregation with baby Jessica, now nearly three months old, and Sister Winnie Mason with Miss Knight beside her. The old lady had said that nothing would keep her away from the wedding of her former pupil to that wonderful doctor, who had not only rescued her from a life of lonely infirmity, but had saved her cat as well.

Anne noted Lady Hylton, trying to make the best of what she considered a rash move on Anne's part.

'Stretbury Memorial just won't be the same without you in residence,' she had sighed. 'And I hear that you are going to live in one of those new flats that used to be the coaching stables of the Horse and Groom—hardly suitable for a doctor and his wife, surely!'

'We're negotiating for a house in Stretford, Lady Hylton,' Anne had assured her, smiling. 'We should be able to move in before the end of the year.'

'I simply can't understand why you seem to be in such a hurry,' Margaret had said. 'After all, you've known him less than six months!'

Anne had assured her that the marriage was based on a firm foundation of mutual love and understanding, and that neither of them wished to delay it a day longer than was necessary and now even Lady Hylton was convinced by the happiness she saw in the eyes of them both.

And now the wedding-day had come and Anne held her head high as she went forward to take this man's hand in hers for life. Her memory roved back to that evening in March when she had eyed the tall stranger with a certain suspicion. Could she have dimly realised then that she was face to face with her destiny, the man who had come to release her from the restraints of the past? The unforgiveness in her heart that had affected her outlook and made her shun the thought of marriage had now melted away in the blessed warmth of Conor's love. By his patient understanding he had taught her to live more fully, and from now on their lives would merge to share whatever joys or burdens came their way. She knew that life with Conor McGuire would sometimes be exasperating, and they still had a lot to learn from each other, but it would never be dull, and there would always be laughter. . .

The look in the bridegroom's eyes as he took Anne's hand told everybody present that this was the culmination of his hopes and dreams from the day of his first meeting with her. He had seen the beauty beneath the bristling efficiency, the desirable and sensual woman enclosed in the ivory tower of her professional life by the hurt of her father's desertion—the father she had learned to pity and forgive as love had unlocked the prison of the past.

The good wishes and congratulations of their families and many friends echoed round the hospital boardroom where the reception was being held, and where Conor was prevailed upon to give the traditional speech.

'My wife and I wish you all as happy as we are today, though I still can't believe that I've gone and married the Senior Nursin' Administrator,' he told them, to an accompaniment of laughter and applause. 'I bless the day I arrived here in Stretbury, but——'

He caught Matthew Crawford's eye and gave him a knowing wink.

'But sure, it's goin' to be hard for a man to live up to, bein' married to an indispensable woman—just the luck o' the Irish!'

And he kissed his blushing bride once again.

"All it takes is one letter to trigger a romance"

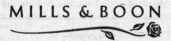

To celebrate 10 years of Temptation we are giving away a host of tempting prizes...

10th All you have to do is complete the wordsearch puzzle below and send it to us by 31 May 1995.

The first 10 correct entries drawn from the bag will each win 12 month's free supply of exciting Temptation books (4 books every month with a total annual value of around £100).

The second 10 correct entries drawn will each win a 200g box of *Thorntons* Temptations chocolates.

I	F	G	N	I	T	I	C	X	E
A	O	X	O	C	A	I	N	S	S
N	O	I	T	A	T	P	M	E	T
N	B	V	E	N	R	Y	N	X	E
I	R	O	A	M	A	S	N	Y	R
V	C	M	T	I	U	N	N	F	U
E	O	H	U	O	T	M	V	E	T
R	N	X	U	R	E	Y	S	I	N
S	L	S	M	A	N	F	L	Y	E
A	T	O	N	U	T	R	X	L	V
R	U	O	M	U	H	I	A	A	D
Y	W	D	Y	O	F	I	M	K	A

TEMPTATION	ROMANTIC
SEXY	SENSUOUS
FUN	ADVENTURE
EXCITING	HUMOUR
TENTH	ANNIVERSARY

PLEASE TURN OVER FOR ENTRY DETAILS

MILLS & BOON

HOW TO ENTER

10⁴ All the words listed overleaf below the wordsearch puzzle, are hidden in the grid. You can find them by reading the letters forward, backwards, up and down, or diagonally. When you find a word, circle it or put a line through it.

Don't forget to fill in your name and address in the space below then put this page in an envelope and post it today (you don't need a stamp). Closing date 31st May 1995.

Temptation Wordsearch,
FREEPOST,
P.O. Box 344,
Croydon,
Surrey
CR9 9EL

COMP395

Are you a Reader Service Subscriber?   Yes ☐   No ☐

Ms/Mrs/Miss/Mr _____

Address _____

_____

_____ Postcode _____

One application per household. You may be mailed with other offers from other reputable companies as a result of this application.
Please tick box if you would prefer
not to share in these opportunities. ☐